Allahabad Aria

Neelum Saran Gour is a professor of English literature at Allahabad University and a well-known writer. She has authored eight works of fiction and edited a pictorial volume on the history and culture of the city of Allahabad. She is also the author of the non-fiction work *Three Rivers and a Tree: The Story of Allahabad University*. Her critical writings and short fiction have been included in various anthologies. She has been a humour columnist for the Allahabad page of the *Hindustan Times* and a book reviewer for *The Indian Review of Books* and *The Times Literary Supplement*, UK. To know more about her, visit www.neelumsarangour.com

Allahabad Aria

Stories about Allahabad

NEELUM SARAN GOUR

RUPA

Published by
Rupa Publications India Pvt. Ltd 2015
7/16, Ansari Road, Daryaganj
New Delhi 110002

Sales Centres:
Allahabad Bengaluru Chennai
Hyderabad Jaipur Kathmandu
Kolkata Mumbai

ISBN: 978-81-291-3659-6

First impression 2015

10 9 8 7 6 5 4 3 2 1

The moral right of the author has been asserted.

Printed by Parksons Graphics Pvt. Ltd, Mumbai

To all those, scattered across the continents,
to whom the name Allahabad means a chapter of home

Contents

ONE

Southern Cross

It was the Sabharwal kids, Rahul and Naina, who first began calling him Trishanku. Till then he'd been plain Bablu. He had a regular name, of course, the one in the school register, Raghav. But he didn't think of himself as Raghav. Only as Bablu and later as Trishanku. In the years to come he would sometimes come to be called Shanku, followed by a stylish Trish, but that was years away.

He remembered the afternoon when the name descended on him like the mantle of a perverse king, which indeed the Trishanku in the fable was, a king. In later years, on the few occasions that they happened to run into one another, Rahul and Naina and he, they did not mention that winter of '88. Rahul had been eight, Naina seven and he, Bablu, had been five. Rahul, precocious, had been scaring them with stories about 'ghosts and ghostesses', leaving Bablu enormously impressed. Then he had picked up a ragged *Amar Chitra Katha* and humorously gone on to draw a perceptive if somewhat unfeeling correspondence between Bablu's situation and the legendary Trishanku's.

'So he hangs there, just like that. All upside-down, *ulta-pulta*, feet up, head down, in his *ulta-pulta* heaven, neither here nor there, this Trishanku.'

This Trishanku who wanted to ascend to heaven in his mortal body.

'Like you sometimes stay with us and sometimes with your Papa and sometimes with your Aunties and Uncles and sometimes with your Grandpa. Not like us two who always stay in one place, in one house, with one Daddy and one Mummy.'

For indeed, whenever his parents had a big scene, a nomadic existence had followed.

An upside-down heaven had to be hell or it may just have been a heaven in an inverse dimension. Hanging in the astral outer reaches of the universe, seeing everything upside-down, going all wrong-headed. The great sage Vashishtha had refused to grant Trishanku the power to visit heaven in his physical body but that other great sage, Vishvamitra, had agreed. But the gods protested. A law could not be broken, no, not even by yogic decree of a great spiritual master. Still, a promise is a promise. So Vishvamitra made Trishanku an alternate heaven and he hangs there still, a star. It is called the Southern Cross, said learned Rahul. It hangs upside down— neither here nor there.

'Like a *dhobi ka gadha*,' Rahul had idiomatically enlarged the conception to facilitate better comprehension of his own situation to Bablu and with no malicious intent. A washerman's donkey belongs neither to the home nor to the river-bank but plods from one to the other, ever homeless.

And that dhobi's donkey had led on to the delightful

animal-sayings game. Why do we have such funny sayings about animals in Hindi? Rahul had mused, his hyperactive brain taking a quantum leap into another matter of acute interest. Then they'd sat remembering comic animal sayings in Hindi : *Kutte ki poonch kabhi seedhi nahin hoti*—a dog's curly tail can never be straightened; *sau-sau choohe khai ke, billi chali haj karne*—having swallowed hundreds of mice, the cat now goes on pilgrimage; *geedar ki maut aati hai to woh sheher ki taraf bhagta hai*—the jackal doomed to die runs stupidly towards the city; *uunt ke muh mein zeera*—a cumin seed in a camel's mouth; *museebat padne par gadhe ko bhi baap banana padta hai*—in times of misfortune even the ass must be adopted as a father; *bandar kya jaane adrak ka swaad*—what does a monkey know of the flavour of ginger!

Bablu loved those afternoons at the Sabharwal's house in Kanpur. He spent four hours with them while Papa was at the factory. The Sabharwal Auntie-Uncle were kind. The Auntie cooked nice things and the Uncle patted him on the head and called him 'chhutanku'—funny little one, a nickname that might even have been a sonic parody of Trishanku. But between the ice creams and the snacks and the stories and games, they kept asking him cautious questions. What did Papa do in the evenings? He cooked dinner, he sat over Bablu's homework, he went to the bazaar to buy fruit and things like crepe paper for Bablu's school project, he watched cricket matches and films on TV. All this Bablu managed to convey more or less credibly.

'Does he...does he drink?' asked the Auntie timidly, casting a sidelong glance at her husband.

'Yes,' said Bablu. 'He drinks Rooh Afza and Limca and

lots and lots of tea out of a flask. He also drinks water from the fridge.'

'That's enough, Malti,' Uncle Sabharwal silenced his concerned wife.

'But tea...why tea?' she was perplexed.

'They often do that. Well, it's good for them I'm sure.'

And one other question that sometimes came up was: 'Chhutanku, d'you remember your mother's name?'

'Yes. Mummy.' He always answered.

'I mean her real name.'

'Mummy,' he insisted. He stressed the middle ems as Indians do, so that it sounded like Mum-Mee. For some mysterious reason he pretended not to know that name. Sarita. Which much later he learnt meant Little River.

She could not have had a more visually appropriate name to him, she who'd become one with the river. When the urn with the ashes was tipped over the edge of the boat at the Sangam in Allahabad, the water turned charcoal slick. The cloudy pollen of ash scattered on the water, turning it scaly like the back of a fish, before the fine web of its feathery spray spread swiftly on the water as each particle of floating ash went dancing away from all the others in reckless disbanding of self until nothing was left in the waves lapping quietly against the side of the boat.

Bablu had been in the boat, with Big Grandpa Dadaji and Papa and Big Uncle Pitambar and Middle Uncle Vijai and Small Uncle Akshay. It was the first time he saw Papa smoking cigarette after cigarette in Dadaji's presence, it being a custom in old Indian families to hide the cigarette in the presence of an elder. Bablu was interested in the little brown stubs that

Papa tossed into the water as he chain-smoked. They went floating in giddy half-circles along with the shredded jasmines that had garlanded the urn, unspooling a thin, streaky trail of brown murk in the water. Papa's full eyes stared, dazed, at the distant bridge as the boat slipped quietly back. He looked like a great tragic hero in a movie. All through the ten days of ritual segregation, he had sat beside Papa on a wattle mat beside the urn and the burning lamp, its wick kept ever oiled and lit. There had been such solidarity of silence between them. Together they had gone to pour water in the earthen pot dangling from the peepal tree's branch so that Mummy's soul could come and sip water if she liked. Instead he saw sparrows dipping their beaks. That was why, when Papa and he were back in Kanpur, where Papa worked, they continued to feed sparrows on the terrace.

And after Papa's head had been ritually shaved and the nails cut and the Aunties were allowed to oil and comb their hair and get out of mourning wear, the whole extended family had congregated for Papa's rasam-pagri. How handsome Papa looked, seated cross-legged on a wooden platform with a new turban ceremonially placed on his head, as brothers, brothers-in-law, uncles-by-marriage, cousins-by-old-village-kinship and elders of the family came one by one to put the tilak on his forehead and offer new clothes and money. Papa looked like Lord Rama at his coronation, thought Bablu, gazing awestruck, at his father and also revelling in the attention of the guests who let him stick chewing gum on their cars and hide their footwear and only said, 'Ah, poor child, poor little thing.'

When the Who-Is-To-Look-After-Bablu? question came up, everyone in the family offered, insisted. It almost turned into a courtroom custodial issue, Dadaji presiding.

But Papa said not a word.

'Try to understand,' reasoned Auntie Neeta, 'he'll be so much more comfortable in a proper home. Regular meals, regular hours. And my kids will be good company for him. A good influence too. Very well brought-up kids they are too—everyone says so.' Here a faint micro-suggestion had stolen in that he, Bablu, was not well brought up—so far— but would enjoy the advantages of a good upbringing if he moved in with her family.

'And he is always welcome to stay with us,' put in Uncle Vijai after checking out his wife Ruchi's assenting nod. 'In fact we've always wanted a son and my two little girls will be so pleased to have him around.'

'As for us,' said Auntie Seema, 'You know how it is with us.' (Auntie Seema and Uncle Akshay had no children.) 'We'd feel blest if a little child became part of our family.'

'I'm due to retire in another four months,' said Dadaji, who was a Judge in the District Court at Allahabad, 'so I shall have all the time in the world for a grandchild.'

But Papa sat stony-faced, his eyes still absent, as though he heard none of this.

'Be sensible, Bhai Sahab,' continued Auntie Neeta. 'A child needs companions his age. Someone to sit over his homework. Someone to tell him stories. Someone to set an example. Be a role model. Not...' She left her sentence incomplete but the sense was quite evident. Not someone like you. Irresponsible. Unreliable.

'Besides,' said Auntie Seema, 'it's too early to be saying this, forgive me, but sooner or later you will marry again and who knows how your wife will take to this child. You'll have more children. God willing...'

Papa scorched her with a furious look. 'Shut up,' he muttered in a low voice, his brow clenched. She drew in her breath with a hiss and shut up, looking injured.

Uncle Akshay said, 'I think someone should ask the kid. Who would you like to stay with, Bablu?'

He had turned and pointed at Papa. Then Papa raised his head and looked him full in the face. His glazed eye cleared and there was in them a coming-alive, a making-sense, as he looked at the small, pointing finger, unshaking, sure. A magic staff dividing the sea, making the waves roll away, clearing a path.

That evening Papa asked Bablu what he wanted most. Bablu said he wanted to go on a boat. He'd been told there were dolphins in the river. Papa said fine, boats if you say so.

There were no dolphins. Instead there were birds and more birds. Papa said they'd come all the way from Siberia to the Sangam. Their large, white wings came flapping the air above their boat like the wings of a host of archangels. Bablu wondered if Papa would take out a bottle from his hip pocket, as he often did, and start taking big swigs. Then his eyes would bulge, his face would grow red and the veins stand out on his temples. What if the boatman got drunk too and their boat just drifted down, down, down the Ganga. Leaving Allahabad far behind, drifting past Benaras and Kolkata and down into the Indian Ocean towards Africa and the South Pole. Bablu knew the shape of the land masses and the rivers and seas from the big plastic globe he got as a birthday gift when he turned five. But Papa did not take out a bottle.

Instead he produced a little comb. Bending over the side of the country boat, he dipped his hand in the water and wet Bablu's spiky hair. Then he parted it carefully and drew the comb down it. The hair sprang back in spikes again.

'Now you comb mine,' said Papa.

Bablu stared. 'You've got no hair, Papa,' he said.

'Comb it all the same,' smiled Papa.

So Bablu, puzzled, scraped the comb up and down Papa's bristly crown, patting down the prickly scalp with his small firm paws. Papa made him do it again and again as though he liked that small, firm touch there.

'When will your hair grow back, Papa?'

It was just a sort of polite conversational query but the boatman laughed and broke into a song: *Maiyya kab-hi badhegi choti?* Then he explained the song to Bablu. This was Lord Krishna as a little child asking his mother, fretfully, when, when will my pigtail grow? A baby god with a pigtail? Bablu laughed outright and Papa smiled in amusement. The boatman said the song was made up by a blind poet hundreds of years ago, and he went on to sing another of the blind poet's songs.

'Prabhu more avguna chit na dharo...
Lord, do not look on my faults,
You, who are known as the One
Who sees all things with equal eye.
Your grace can row me across.
One piece of iron is used in worship,
Another in the butcher's steel
The philosopher's stone sees neither merit nor fault
But changes them both to purest gold...'

Papa took the comb back, put it in his pocket but kept holding on to Bablu's hand.

'You and I,' he started saying, but his voice went all squelchy and his eyes went strange and he stopped... 'and no one else,' he managed to say. But Bablu understood what he meant.

And the boatman, who had seen or heard none of this, went on rowing, singing on:

'One is called river, another a murky drain.
When they mingle they become one colour
And are known as Sursari, river of gods...'

Sursari! Sarita. Little river.

'This time take me across, or give up your promise to save...'

The Siberian cranes dipped and swooped, archangels on the wing.

Six months, the family had whispered. Maybe ten. It actually lasted about a year, when people had actually begun using the word 'miracle' and thanking the gods and the stars. But what had to happen, happened suddenly. Just one ordinary day, without portent or advance notice.

He heard Papa stride heavily up the stairs. Heard the door to the living room creak open. He heard Papa call: 'Bablu.' He saw Papa reach into the pocket of his baggy trousers for his wallet and noticed the unusual fumble in the way his thick, blunt fingers took out the money.

'Two packs of Goldflake,' he told Bablu, thrusting the rupee notes into his hand without catching his eye. His voice was slightly nasal, phlegm-soggy.

Bablu stood there, not getting what Papa was driving at. Papa raised his eyes and there was a flare of manic challenge sparking in the depths of the pupils, something that brought a panic of old images shrilling to life in Bablu's mind.

'Go, you little bastard! Go!' said Papa in a low, charged voice, heavy with menace. 'Go!'

He gave Bablu a little push. The street lights had gone off in the evening power cut, the road plunged in simmering darkness. Bablu stood uncertainly in front of the door. Then Papa came stumbling towards him and in the same instant Bablu's legs unlocked and he sprang out of reach as he'd seen Mummy do long ago. There was a scowl on Papa's face, the forehead muscles all bunched up. His nose seemed thicker, broader, and his eyelids were puffy. And when Bablu said: 'No, you go, Papa,' a large, square fist had crashed into the side of his head, then unclenched to grab the collar of his T-shirt and flung him about, squealing like a terrified pup, slamming into walls, table corners, sending a lamp tottering and a glass jug crashing in a rain of shards. Until, frantic, Bablu made it to the front door, undid the bolts and ran into the corridor and hammered on the Sabharwal's door and scratched at it with his small nails, his voice lifted in a shrill, screaming gabble, as hiccups jerked his throat about and shudders convulsed his thin frame.

The door had opened and the Auntie-Uncle had pulled him in. All he could utter in his hiccup-jerking whimper was 'Papa...'

They understood immediately and pulled him in and drew the bolts on the bulky form that had lumbered up to the door, slurring drowsy abuse.

When Bablu's shivers had stilled and his incoherent blubber had died down, when the sound of hammering fists and clumping feet on the landing had gone and a distant door had banged shut, Sabharwal Uncle made a late-night phone call to Dadaji in Allahabad. By the next afternoon Big Uncle Pitambar had arrived to take Bablu back with him. When Bablu stole in, clutching Sabharwal Uncle's hand tightly in his own, Papa was awake, sitting hunched up at the dining table, his head in his hands. Big Uncle Pitambar was speaking in a loud, constant, disgusted monotone. Papa did not look at Bablu even once. But as the taxi reversed in the yard below, Bablu saw, through the tinted glass of the rolled-up window, Papa's befogged face at the first floor balcony, his hair all tossed and tousled, looking down bleary-eyed, with a sleepy expression in his face as though he was there and not there. Another Trishanku.

So Bablu stayed with all the aunts and uncles by turns, ably living up to his reputation as the all-wrong kid, the problem child with the upside-down brain. Auntie Neeta learnt that she couldn't quite bring him up right or be a role model because he seemed impervious to any refining influence. Soon Bablu found himself staying with Uncle Vijai and Auntie Ruchi and their two little daughters and in next to no time the little girls began living in mortal terror, having been turned into objects of such ungovernable violence that the doctor had to be called. By this time Auntie Seema and Uncle Akshay had moved to the South and pleaded school admission issues and it fell to Dadaji to devote his retirement leisure to something other than reading the paper in the front verandah or engaging in passionate political harangue with his morning walk friends. He soon realized that calming a perverse kid was unlike calling a noisy courtroom to order.

When the entire family got together for Diwali, the Bablu Question came up for much-whispered discussion. More so because Bablu's father was expected too, a bit of information that Bablu registered with listless apathy.

Papa arrived. For a rest, said Auntie Neeta, because he was sick, though the word 'sacked' also figured in the whispered conversations. His face looked sunken and haggard by daylight but swarthy and bloated indoors so that it was hard to say whether he was fatter or thinner. He looked both at the same time, lumpy, pasty-faced and pallid, his feet swollen to large loaves of flesh, his belly big and protuberant but his shoulders sagging in his loose, shabby shirts.

Bablu kept out of his way as much as he could. On the first day he caught the flash of eagerness in Papa's bilious eyes and the quick turn of the head when Bablu darted across his line of vision. But when he called to him, Bablu sped away. There proceeded a silent hide-and-seek game between the two. If Papa sat down to eat at the dining table, Bablu contrived to carry his plate into the garden. If Papa came and sat at his bedside, Bablu only shut his eyes more tightly and pretended to be asleep. It couldn't go on for long, though. On the third evening Papa called to him: 'Bablu, come and press my feet.' Recalling to mind, an old nightly ritual when Bablu had squeezed the ache out of Papa's heels and toes and also tickled the instep and roared with laughter, that enchanted winter that seemed so long ago.

There was nothing for it but to comply. Papa's feet were mottled and bloated and little craters appeared where Bablu, head hanging, dug in his fingers. But Papa lay with eyes closed, as though all he wanted was the touch of those fingers. Suddenly he opened his eyes and looked closely at Bablu. It was not a mistake—Bablu was digging his sharp little nails into the puffy flesh, trying to hurt, to pierce the sick skin and claw at the flesh until it winced in pain. It happened again and then again. Papa drew up his legs and said with a peculiar catch in his voice: 'Enough now. Go and play.'

Now that his father was home, there had to be a reckoning.

'Look to your son, mister,' said Uncle Vijai satirically as he led Bablu in by the ear and stood him in front of Papa. 'I just caught him sticking burning sparklers into the calves's backs. Branding them. The grocer has been murmuring about catching him red-handed, picking up things. My daughter was pushed from a banister down three levels and fractured her arm, so I say, look to your son. He's your responsibility too.'

Papa rose wearily and took hold of Bablu's other ear, swivelled him round and smacked his cheek.

'You little bastard!' he said in a voice that, even to Bablu's ear, sounded defeated. 'Let me see you doing this sort of thing again and I'll shove a burning sparkler up your arse!'

Having fulfilled his obligations as a parent expected to administer disciplinary correction, he let go of Bablu.

But the very next morning the family servant Nathu Lal came complaining that his savings were missing from the box which he kept in his room.

'This monster-child!' cried Auntie Neeta, 'To steal from a servant! Bhai Sahab,' she turned to Papa. 'Give this problem a thought, will you?'

So Papa lurched out of his chair and fell on Bablu, landing

slaps and cuffs and pummels, aiming them always in such strategic ways that the blows struck home out of the onlookers' range of vision and shielded by his own bulky frame. And that's when Bablu began suspecting that Papa was either too feeble now or else only acting. Pretending to beat him for the satisfaction of the others but keeping the blows very gentle. He himself fell into the spirit of the charade and bawled louder than he felt, getting into the act. And later, when the hue and cry had died down, Papa lumbered up to where Bablu was scrawling on the verandah wall with a stub of crayon, put his hand on his head and said those words again: 'You and I…and no one else.' Words which sent a little stir riffling through Bablu's heart.

This happened again. When Auntie Seema's dress, drying on the clothesline in the yard, was discovered mysteriously ripped to ribbons, the charade was enacted again. Lots of shouting and banging about, lots of bawling and at the end of it all, those words, sealing a sacred covenant of sorts.

Money kept vanishing all the same. 'No one can do a thing for this boy,' Dadaji shook his head sadly. 'I'm doing my best, God knows, but I'm filled with such helplessness. When I think of my old dog Tipu and the way a cracker was tied to his tail and set alight and the terrible burns on the poor creature's back…And yesterday it was Nathu's money, today it is Akshay's. Bablu, look at me. Did you take money out of the pocket of Uncle Akshay's trousers when he hung them up in the bathroom? Did you?'

But Bablu had mastered a style of smiling that was altogether seraphic. Disarming, fixed, as though the questions came in an alien language. So, apart from the slaps and ear-pullings and arm-twistings, there were head-pattings and counselling sessions and horoscope examinations and consultations with the old family priest and someone even brought the phone number of a child psychologist.

On the last day of the Diwali holidays Big Uncle Pitambar, groping under the cotton mattress in his room where he'd taken to hiding his purse, found his entire Diwali bonus missing.

'This is the absolute limit!' he rushed to the drawing room, thunder on his brow. 'This child has stretched our tolerance to breaking point. We can't go on like this, saying poor kid, poor kid! We've got a little criminal here!'

Then Uncle Vijai went out, looking for Bablu. He returned in a short while, propelling Bablu ahead of him with one hand and in his other hand he held a quarter bottle of Triple X rum. He held up the bottle.

'The seal is broken. He was at the garden tap. Topping it up with water. No doubt he knows the dilution. Starting young!'

There was a general gasp. Papa had started up in his chair. In two strides he was by Bablu's side. His scalding gaze travelled from Bablu to the bottle. He bent low so that his face was at a level with Bablu's.

'Open your mouth,' he commanded in a low, strained voice, so dangerously tense that it had turned hoarse. 'Say aaaah-haah. Go on.'

Bablu, drowsy and not-all-there, breathed rum fumes into Papa's face as he said 'Aaah haah.'

Then the real beating started. Such a beating that Aunties and Uncles flew to the child's rescue but Papa seemed insane with rage and would stop at nothing short of murder. Bablu screamed, dodged and ducked, raced shrieking from shut door to divan, from TV stand to china cupboard but Papa had by now taken hold of Dadaji's walking stick and he flailed it about, swung and struck, catching Bablu in the calves, on the back, on the neck, making him howl and roar and cling to the horrified onlookers who strove in vain to shield him from the blows and received a few stinging cuts themselves in the process.

'Bastard!' roared Papa, 'Cur-spawn! Pig whelp! Sister fucker! Drunkard! Drunkard! Drunkard! I'll teach you to drink, you mother fucker, you! Thief! I'll teach you to drink!'

He came stumbling towards Bablu, his eyes boiling, the stick raised above his head like a cobra's poised and readied hood.

'Thief!' he shouted again as the stick descended on the corner of the table as Bablu skipped aside. The stick splintered in two, the table top cracked and Bablu's voice, trembling between breathless gulps of spittle, spoke up in desperate defiance.

'You! Thief!!'

Papa stopped, befuddled by this unexpected counter-assault.

'That is the thief, Big Uncle,' squealed Bablu. 'He took your money. And from Auntie Seema's bag and Nathu's box and Dadaji's purse. He gave it to me. To buy that thing. Every day.' He indicated the bottle on top of the fridge and went on. 'He said...he said "You and me..." Here he began to shake and clung to Dadaji, still pointing accusingly at his father.

His small pointing finger, unshaking, sure, made the tall walls of water come collapsing again to submerge his drowning father in utter, mortified, shamed silence. No one spoke. He saw Papa drop the stick and sink into a chair. Then he saw him rise shakily to his feet, go to his cot in the next room and lie down, drawing up his knees in a foetal curve. He saw him turn away to the wall, his face hidden by his two bent arms. His shoulders heaved in soundless, retching sobs.

Even as a grown man, Trish found it hard, driving over that bridge across the Ganga with the country boats sailing tranquilly in the river below and Siberian cranes in the sky. The sight brought a peculiar lunge in the chest when he recalled his poor drink-sodden father who sank to the depths of disgrace that evening long ago, as a stone sinks to the river's bed. And the mother whose feathery essence disintegrated in the Ganga's waters, racing swiftly downstream. It seemed then that they merged and flowed in his veins as his secret life stream even as the waters of the two rivers did, far beneath.

TWO

The Day I Met My Ideal Reader

*S*ome time around the middle of 2005, a news item appeared in *The Hindu*:

'Pottermania: One lakh copies sold in a single day.' The opening paragraph announced in breathless excitement: 'It doesn't get bigger than this. The latest J.K. Rowling book *Harry Potter and the Half-Blood Prince* has made history by selling over 100,000 copies in a single day in India. The fastest book to fly off the shelves in this country, it sold 139 copies every minute from half past six in the morning to six in the evening on the first day of release this past weekend.' For publishers, bookstores, publicists and market-watchers it was the biggest publishing event ever known and great delight was expressed at what was described as a 'golden' day for bookshops across the country. If that was the kind of sales record all over the world, I presume Ms Rowling was a satisfied and pleased woman that weekend as the figures kept rolling in.

I have enormous respect for Ms Rowling, ever since I read the transcript of her address at Harvard which revealed her to be a scholar of hard-core metaphysical learning beneath her masquerade as the magical entertainer. But there was one person whose delight that weekend possibly exceeded the collective rejoicings of the publishing world and that was me. I had sold 25 copies of a self-published book across a counter at my first-ever book launch that I had coaxed, cajoled and pressured into happening by dint of sheer personal nuisance-making at a well-known bookshop (hereinafter called The Bookshop) at a well-known Civil Lines restaurant (hereinafter called The Venue.)

To rewind to the backstory, I was, in 2005, a five-book author, ably supported by my publishers, and with no earthly reasons to self-publish. Maxine Hong Kingston wrote somewhere that a writer's age must not be calculated in calendar years but rather in writing years. Now in 2005 if my writing age was calculated in books, I might have been five years old. But if it was calculated in the number of calendar years counting from the date of publication of my first book, it would be thirteen years. And finally if it was reckoned in the number of calendar years since I lisped my first numbers, I guess it would be fifty-ish. If the last, then by 2005 I was a tolerable candidate for a Lifetime Achievement Award, and if the second, I could pass myself off as a debutante literary nymphet. Finally, if my literary age was five, I could still claim the distinction of being a child prodigy! Despite such heartening endorsements of personal standing in the fickle world of letters, I had, circa 2005, developed acute low-esteem issues. I had never, no never, had a book launch. Book launches just didn't happen then in Allahabad. We Allahabadis read of them in the papers and lacerated our hearts with the thought of all that we were missing in life! That's also the time when I cautiously floated a minuscule publishing unit as an insurance against the terrifying prospect of mountains of unpublished manuscripts littering my living spaces, unwanted by any publishers in the grim and unfathomable future. Tentatively I published one of my shelved books which no metropolitan publisher wanted to take on, dismissing me summarily with the question: Who Reads Stuff Like This Now? There was nothing for it now except to go for it myself—publish, launch, distribute, sell, and hope I would live to tell the tale. I have survived the experience and herein hangs the tale.

Like a 'coming out' party for a Victorian young lady there would have to be a launch to present my book to the world. (*See Oxford Desk Thesaurus*, page 284: launch: verb, start [off], set in motion, set or get going, begin, embark upon or on, initiate, inaugurate, originate, establish, organize, found... shoot, fire, discharge, hurl, throw, sling, pitch, fling, catapult... float, set afloat. As in 'We are about to launch a scheme for dockside development.' As in 'The enemy launched ground-to-air missiles against our planes.' Okay, okay, one might be tempted to shut up the Thesaurus and say, I've got the general idea. (These Thesauruses—or should it be Thesaurusii, as in dinosaurus, tyrannosaurus—have this nagging tone of repetition and rubbing-it-in worse than your high-strung mother!)

Living in Middle India (formerly called Mofussil) I was anxious to get the recipe right. Upper-crust Allahabad, always a city that plumed itself on its writers, was only just beginning to fantasize about the classy flavour of the commercial book event, though the old Friday Club of the University or the Muir Hostel Social in the sixties were notable precedents in the exclusive Book of Belonging and our *mushairas* and *kavi sammelans* were the toast of the literary world. The operative word here, please note, is 'commercial'. Book events then were like lit-fests now. There were so many of them. And they were always happening elsewhere.

The ingredients of the recipe for the perfect book-event included a venue, a celebrity, a compere, invites (formerly called invitations), plenty of grog (optional) and grub (compulsory), the presence of the press, a reading by the author, a display of the books piled up in towers or pyramids or high-rises, a sales counter and someone to receive the cash and tear out the receipt and, not least in order of importance, some volunteers not indisposed to part with cash in exchange of said book and till such time as this operation became necessary, to decorate the rows of chairs and suffer the proceedings. The book was to come in all gift-wrapped, like a boar's head with an apple between its teeth. It was to be ceremonially disrobed and exposed to view. And thereafter the author, or someone in good voice, read out a passage or two, not short enough to give the impression of unholy haste, not so long as to set the audience a-fidget.

At this point in my researches I was conscious of a certain fastidious dismay. Why was it necessary to follow this Dance-Of-The-Seven-Veils, Salome-Before-The-Throne-Of-Herod striptease kind of ceremonial unveiling of a perfectly self-respecting book? I believed in thinking out of the box. Why not do things differently? Why not garland the first copy, ring bells and gongs and chant mantras to the clashing of cymbals? Why not smash a bottle of champagne—or a coconut—against its spine? Why not douse it in holy water, anointed with consecrated oil? Or give away the first ten copies to the poor raddiwala in charity? Or tear it up and scatter its soul-essence to the four directions, to become one with the Great Empyrean? My own gesture of celebration, whenever my publishers sent me a packet containing the first copy of one of my books, has been something so chronically, contemptibly mofussil and so amply deserving of the ridicule of the superior sceptic that I blush to confess it. I have always placed it before my place of prayer, such prayer as I do in an eclectic, non-denominational sort of way, and subsequently before a photograph of my parents. Once I bought a box of mithais and had a feast for my stray dogs. But clearly none of this would be good enough now, I decided.

One of my metro-savvy friends resolved to take me in hand and told me all about a launch she'd attended in Mumbai. It was the launch to end all launches, she said. The Bookstore choc-a-bloc with junta. Standing room only. Not one celebrity but five. No, actually one central celebrity, like the sun in the planetary system, and four satellite celebrities. The main attraction was this ravishingly beautiful filmstar whose face had launched a million cameras. The satellites were writers of all shapes and sizes, hues and stripes, some dressed like corporate execs emerging from a Board Meeting, some lounging around looking like Fab India ads, some surprised in the act of changing their costume from Flower Child to Champagne Socialist, and more photographers than book-reading types stampeding about like mustangs on the loose, never mind if everyone forgot the book! You've got to concentrate on the celebs, my friend advised. Five celebs! I was doubtful. No, one twenty-four carat celeb would be good enough seeing that I was on an austerity drive. But how to arrange a celeb?

'Well,' she ventured hesitantly, 'you might consider me.' The dogged self-assurance of the Allahabadi is awesome, growing in direct proportion to the insularity of the candidate! My friend had done a bit role in a TV serial about two decades back.

'I don't want your face launching a million cameras—which is bound to happen if you step in. Remember it's my book I'm launching, not your face.'

If I was inwardly congratulating myself on my finesse I had need of it in the days to come as I went about trying to arrange a celebrity. Several friends volunteered and had to be fended off. It's taken me years to repair those relationships. Eventually a celeb answering to my requirements consented. The invites materialized and were sent. The banner put up. The compeer showed me his poems and asked me to consider publishing them once the present business was over and done with. The Bookstore set up the pyramid of books and installed a brisk assistant behind it. The friends demanded to know whether there'd be anything good to eat and were reassured. The press nibbled and scribbled. My celeb unwrapped my book, the audience clapped, the compeer (who'd gotten acquainted with me only an hour back) uttered his general admiration of me and I sold 25 copies!

As I look back across the mists of time I can see my friends swilling and gorging, slapping me on the back and saying considerately: 'No need to buy, guys, she might fall short of copies and we can always borrow a copy from her if we feel like reading it.' Me standing with my face organized in a flight-stewardess smile, murmuring: 'Thank you for coming and giving us a chance to welcome you here.' I see myself mingling graciously among the multitudes. Honestly there did seem to be multitudes milling around the buffet table now, people I didn't know, all the Bookstore's employees en masse, crowds of children, hordes of people, and I honestly didn't know where they'd sprung from. They seemed to be tucking in with gusto. I see the old couple sitting benignly in the front row telling me: 'Got to wait an hour for our driver who's caught in a traffic jam, so we thought, why not attend this thing, sit down and rest our feet a bit, na?' I see the eloquent Bengali writer who shouted: 'If your writing has energy, it will live!' I see the quiet woman with short iron-grey hair who came up to me with a purchased copy of my book and said: 'Please inscribe it to Mike Ashley.' I blessed Mike Ashley, whoever he was, as I inscribed it. I see the nattily dressed man who'd sped briskly in and found a seat, saying later: 'I live just down the road. Nothing interesting on TV this evening so I thought I'll nip down and see if there's anything going on here.' Most of all I see my Ideal Reader.

Even as I read my opening lines I had spotted him. He appeared to slouch in his chair but he was all attention, frowning slightly to concentrate better when he appeared to miss a word or a phrase, craning forward to catch my epiphanies as they soared and fell. He wore a long, baggy kurta of indefinite hue over flappy pajamas. His critically savvy eyes sifted wearily through my writerly tricks and impostures and reacted with a spring and a bound to what he and I both knew was real. As the minutes progressed I read for him alone, gratified at a grudging nod, disconcerted by a questioning look, spurred on to peaks of performance I had never touched before. As they say in the tabloids, there was such chemistry between us. This was my perfect audience, I realized, overwhelmed. How many years had I plied the pen and tapped the keys that such a one might some day cross my path! And here he was, decoding the alphabet of my dreams, resonating in answer to my soul's ululations, this incredible stranger!

And during the question hour there was no one as engaged, as stirred, as he. I give you a sample of our discourse:

'Madam,' he said, 'I observe that for each of your characters there's a breakthrough—within the parameters of his or her cultural idiom—and this takes the form of a reaching out to a member belonging to a historically oppositional culture. At the same time there is a concurrent strain of self-doubting in your authorial interventions, as though the humanism you say you explore is for you an already contentious and embattled issue.'

'I am only focusing on the particular,' I replied with humility, treading with care. 'My material here is the individual and it is in the individual alone that I put my faith.'

'But isn't that an illusionist feel-good formula, a mould you've got to break?'

'My considered answer to your question is: No. Having indulged an illusion, I'm vindicating it as an ideal. Because vindicating minimally realizable ideals is our only hope.' I pronounced in ringing tones.

The discussions continued at the buffet table.

'In literary matters I am an unashamed conservative,' he told me. 'But I must say that I find your language striking. It holds the old rhythms of tradition but it is effortlessly updated to accommodate contemporary corruptions and topical freedoms.'

And I was just saying 'By golly!' in true high imperial Brit-Allahabadi interjection to myself when the young sales assistant touched me lightly on the elbow, whispering, 'One minute, ma'am.'

'Excuse me,' I said with a will-be-back-in-a-jiffy smile and sailed away to a corner of the buffet area.

'Don't talk to him,' he said flatly. 'He's a fraud.'

'Meaning what?' I was staggered, stupefied, flummoxed, flabbergasted (see Thesaurus).

'Meaning, he's known as the gate-crasher of Civil Lines. One of these non-practising lawyers of the High Court. Goes all over the place. Wherever there's a good spread. Gets past the guards, I don't know how. Even pockets stuff and carries it home for his dinner. We've threatened him with the police but he keeps turning up.'

I looked back, trying to spot my Ideal Reader. He was not to be seen.

THREE

Under The Bodhi Tree

*U*nder the peepal tree sat Sidhu with his tools, mending the axle of the bicycle trolley, and Munji, cobbling shoes. From time to time they vanished into the little shanty behind the tree and worked at something else. At regular intervals they came out and gazed with misgiving at the overcast sky and the tall peepal. Usually it was a jittery tree, its thousand tinfoil leaves bristling to every breath of breeze. But right now it stood stupefied in a premonition of rain.

Munji shot off instructions: 'Mind how you pack in the spice. It's got to be tight-filled, so tight it'll go bang at the smallest knock. In the city we've used petrol but petrol's so expensive now. The stingy louts! If it wasn't all these loans on my head…How many ready to seal? Remember, the paper's got to be folded close. It's got to look like an ordinary cracker. Speed up, boy. Put in twenty-five nail chips and a handful of bottle shards with the sulphur before you do the final stuffing with garam masala.'

Sidhu's village pundit had named him Siddhartha but nobody called him that now. He'd come from elsewhere, you see. As so many had, pouring into Allahabad from surrounding villages, taking over its language and its character. People called Siddhu 'the fool', and he gave Munji good reason for that.

'Munjia,' he had murmured when the deal was struck, 'there's going to be women and kids at the mela...'

But Munji had snapped, 'Serve them right too. What've these folks ever done for the likes of us, the bastards! Stop your fancy talk, girlie-boy, or I'll have to gift you your own front teeth.'

In U.P.'s sprawling outback the villages of Kallukheda, Jaitikikheda, Sisendi and Banthara were famous for their festive crackers. Men came on bikes and cars all the way from Lucknow, Kanpur, Unnao, even Allahabad, and placed their orders weeks in advance. For Ravana burnings or Diwali displays, for New Year parties or lavish weddings. And now even on special cricket match days. Cobbler Munji's seasonal pataka shop in Daraganj had now brought all the wizardry of Sisendi village to this city of fairs and shrines, plying a brisk trade beneath its peepal tree. Every Dashera-Diwali fortnight, for some time now, Sidhu, the cycle repairer, joined in as an extra help for a bit of extra cash. Pataka making had been the local trade in Sisendi and Munji had learnt the art from old Naqvi himself.

After sundown they sometimes displayed their wares for the benefit of new bulk-buyers. Then fountains of light charged up into the sky and shattered against the stars. Parasols of light opened wide and closed. Brain-blasting cracker-bombs stunned the air and left the leaves of the peepal convulsed with shock. And surging wheels hissed and spat upon the ground, spraying shavings and parings of light all around. People stopped in the middle of what they were doing and stood still to watch this play of empowered chemicals. The white-flower fountains lay sleeping in their sealed earthenware orbs as giant trees lie waiting in minuscule seeds. Pomegranates—anaars, they're called here—earthen globes packed tight with promised flame. The white-flower anaars were created from sulphur, aluminium chips and lime. The red-flower ones from cast-iron dust. And the gold-flower ones from coal dust, magnesium grains and soda. The rockets were mainly powder. Bombs there were, numbered one, two, fifteen and sixty, according to size and sound capacity. And one other kind there was, the one with the garam masala smuggled in, innocent looking and unnamed. They'd be jumbled in with the rest, sealed into packets ear-marked for sale in populous bazaars. Someone had come, late one night in a white Maruti van, and paid in advance for those. Paid extra, much more money than Munji had ever seen in his life, much more than all the others, the white-flower, red-flower, gold-flower anaars could earn in a single season. Making Munji's laugh acquire a brackish sting of bravado since.

'A couple hundred bombs shall brighten up this Dashera for sure. Blast up more Ravans than the curs can handle. Who's there?'

A cyclist had appeared with a misshapen bike, its rear wheel slightly folded and its dented mudguard askew.

'What happened? Accident?' The customer nodded and looked up at the waxen sky. His clothes were wet. 'God's raining there,' he said. 'It's blowing up this way. Water this high.'

'Well, he'd better give us a miss,' said Munji. 'Bad for

business when he rains out of time.' Sidhu undid the bolts, picked up his hammer and pecked away at the dented steel. And as he worked the familiar noontime visitor turned up, whining, 'A paisa, my sons, God repay you. A paisa, may you prosper. A paisa, may your kids live on...'

Munji guffawed. 'I've got no perishing kids, bugger you! And how's that foul-smelling throat, stink-pot? Ugly lump. Smells to high heaven.' He held his nose. 'Filthy sores, phoof!'

And Sidhu thought to himself: 'What must it be like to be so ill, your own folks give you the boot?' He fished out a coin and tossed it into the outstretched claw. 'Here, take yourself off, stink-pot.' He looked up, considering the aluminium light. 'It'll start pouring soon. Where d'you sleep when it rains?'

'At the bus-stop-wallah temple,' croaked the ugly creature.

'Then, be off,' said Munji and Sidhu thought: 'If I were to fall ill like that....' And a shudder of fright passed over him. The same sort of prickly panic that brought him fleeing from the Banda police all the way to Allahabad.

At his Banda district school he'd copied his way up to class nine under the kindly eye of the village teacher. He couldn't make it through the Board exam because he'd been provided the wrong notes to copy. He'd lambasted the teacher bloke, howling: 'That's what you do when you give a caste-brother discount, saala?' He'd started work in his father's fields, helping to grow ganja and bhang in the middle of their vegetable patches right under the nose of the police and the excise departments. But when some caste enemies brought a police inspector along and about a quintal of green ganja plants were recovered from his father's fields and the four adjacent fields, he was picked up by the police, along with six others, and tortured in the lock-up. Ah, those soul-flaying three days! Just thinking of them made his stomach contract and his throat go dry and his tongue turn to dry sack-cloth. He tried not to think of that time but often in his dreams fragments of the old horror reappeared and he awoke with his heart drumming and couldn't get back to sleep. Three days it had been, three excruciating lifetimes, until some phone calls came from someone to someone and then from someone to someone else in the District Headquarters and from that someone else to the mobile phone of the thanedar and by dusk all six undertrials were let off to limp back home, though two of them needed a cart to get back and one kept stopping to vomit blood every hour or so. They got home and the villages of Tera, Panthara, Trisuma, Keotara and Kallee ka Purva resumed their ganja-bhang cultivation. But he, Siddhu, ran away, leaving family, village and work. Just boarded a bus at the district depot and fled to Allahabad, with his mother's silver anklets hidden in his rexine shoulder bag beside his change of clothes and bidis and pack of puffed rice and his little pocket icon of Sankat Mochan Hanuman. Now he sat in Daraganj, a cycle repairer by trade and Munji's seasonal help at festival time. He had no complaints because cycle work came and the part-time fireworks trade took care of the extras. His only problem was the fear which overcame him senselessly many times a week, fear of everything small or big. The world was sown with terror, every moment mined with dread.

At noon they stopped work and went down the road for a bit. There was a mugful of scalding tea every day at old

Haribilas's tea shop. They found the old bag-of-bones squatting on his frail haunches, studying something intently on the floor.

'What's up, old timer?' Munji greeted him.

'See this,' quavered Haribilas. 'It moved. Ah, poor mite. Flew in and dashed against the blades of my ceiling fan.' His withered old man's claw turned the bleeding sparrow over, hovered in tremulous concern over the half-severed wing. He pursed his limp mouth in a feeble pucker of pity, trying to align the wing right, the tormented sparrow quivering in agony.

'Stop. Don't touch that thing.'

Haribilas's gnarled talon stopped short. 'Why?'

'I said don't touch it! Birds carry sickness now. They can make you burn with fever and cough and cough till you cough your shit out and die. I heard on the news.'

Haribilas's laugh was a creaky cackle. 'Rubbish,' he said and turning the poor creature over ever so gently, he lifted it on a paper and carried it to the pitcher in the corner. He dipped the brass ladle into the depths of the pitcher and bringing out a cupful of water, dropped it little by little into the sparrow's mouth. He spilt a great deal, wetting the bird, and mopped the ground with his shoulder cloth, making a mess. 'No Ganga water for you, brother mine,' he quavered. 'This'll have to see you across.'

'Om shanti, shanti, shanti,' scoffed Munji when the bird lay still and Sidhu went all silent and wondered: 'What am I so scared of? I wanted to reach out and touch old stink-pot but I was afraid. I am afraid of a dying bird. Ah, there's fear in everything, such fear that your heart freezes at what may happen to you.' He looked at old Haribilas, his loose sponge-mouth, his sunken-bag eyes, his neck like a scrawny hag-chicken's and he thought: 'What must it be like to be that old?'

Then back to the peepal tree and the shanty and the secret job. The afternoon shade had shrunk to a moist stain and the air was porous with heat. Hammer and clang, hammer and clang, went Sidhu while Munji worked within. Until the nostrils twitched and the suspicion of a sickly-sweet incense assailed the sense, stirring a pang. Munji stuck his head out and grimaced.

'Ugh! Just our bloody luck, mate. A funeral now. Comes of living in Daraganj near the burning ghat, that's what. Who's it? Ah, old dame Phooldevi that kept the gram stall. They've got her all decked up in red. A holy wife, what? My word, marigold garlands too! What a laugh. The poor blighted crone never wore a decent saree all her living days and there she goes, decked out like a new bride! The fools. Well, God rest her soul and may she not reincarnate to sell worm-eaten gram and spend her days a-quibble and a-haggle, ha, ha! May the rain spare her carcass and the logs of her pyre and may she burn well...'

Siddhu trembled at Munji's gumption. 'Don't talk like that,' he whispered. 'The dead can hear.' The thought of Phooldevi's haggard shade standing close beside him sent a chill down his neck and he thought, 'Who knows, she might be right here. What must it be like to lie there dead?'

The funeral procession went by. And one man detached himself from the crowd and came to stand in front of the shanty and the bicycle stall. And Siddhu's heart leapt into his mouth as he took in the police uniform.

'Now then, Munjia,' Daraganj Thana's Sub-Inspector

Yadav blustered. 'It's late by a week.'

'Please give us a little more time, hujoor,' appealed Munji. 'We'll have the cash ready by tomorrow evening.'

'Make it snappy then,' snarled Yadav. 'You wouldn't like to go breathe the sweet lock-up air now, would you? And by the way, I know exactly what you bitch-born curs have been up to.'

Anything in a police uniform made Siddhu's breath go frayed and ragged. His hands shook as he tinkered at the axle of the wheel he was working on. A blunt hunk of boot planted itself on Munji's shoe-stand. 'Here, let's have a good lick of polish.'

Munji applied himself to the foot with slavish attention while Siddhu worked hard to achieve invisibility as far as possible. It was as Munji had given the final slap of the brush on the now mirror-bright leather that another foot appeared beside the policeman's boot. It was a long, lean foot, encased in a torn sandal and a voice spoke: 'A strap for this sandal, son.'

Their eyes travelled up along the tall, robed form and the policeman's voice suddenly turned unctuous. 'Namaskar, Swamiji. His Holiness going to take his dip in the Sangam very late today, Swamiji. Or is it the Nag Vasuki mela?'

The holy man, his matted locks dangling about his face, stood against the afternoon sun and in the glare Siddhu could not see the lines of his face, only his calm, firm foot, neither frail nor muscular, in the rough thongs of the sandal. He did not dare to look straight at the policeman's form but his ears did not fail to catch the note of fawning submission, and he thought: 'What must it be like to be so still and so straight?'

When he looked up again the saffron-clad figure had

paid up and left. So had the policeman. But somehow he'd drawn strength to voice his old doubt again: 'There's going to be women and kids in those melas, Munjia...'

'Shut your mouth and get on with you! And don't forget to pack in the flint and the shards with the spice,' growled Munji in a fit.

But Siddhu already knew what to do and he did it while straightening a nail under the hammer. The hammer came crashing down on his thumb and he let out a howl of pain. The hot, sticky blood erupted on the anvil. Tears smarted in his eyes. But there was relief in his swarthy face.

'Hé Ram!' he gasped. 'This hand's done for. You do your garam masala crackers yourself, bhaiya.'

'Saala!' swore Munji. 'Did you have to smash your dog-paw now?' Then he frowned. 'Don't you run away with the idea that you're out of this. You're the one that's got to carry the stuff down in the trolley to Abdul's garage tomorrow evening and bring back the cash. Your hand's gone to the furnace but you can cycle alright.'

Siddhu's heart sank as he thought: 'There's no getting out of this.' And waves of fear broke against his brain.

But was there really no opting out? He wondered as he pedalled the trolley slowly down the highway in the smoky dusk. If instead of taking the big, wrapped cartons down to Abdul's garage, he took the next turn and cycled three kilometres more and just left the stuff at the police post and ran away? But the very thought of the police made him go breathless. They'd put needles under his fingernails. They'd hung him upside-down. They'd lashed his back with leather belts. He remembered the burning sting of the big, brass buckle. No, better to turn back and head straight for Abdul's.

But he set his teeth and said: 'No, not a brute of a small-time police-wallah. I'll cycle down to the Bara-Sahib's bungalow.' He had asked the way. He had packed his rexine bag again, cycle repair tools and all, and would never return to Munji's again. He would leave the trolley near the gate of the Commissioner's bungalow on the broad, green road to Teliarganj, stroll off for a pee and then bolt across the field into the market behind and make for the railway station. But when he came within sight of the Commissioner's bungalow, his heart began drumming out its dread so loud he could feel his whole chest quake. There were two uniformed sentries in a sentry-box at the gate. The sight of their uniform made his stomach turn. In the lock-up he'd been made to drink the urine of his tormentors. His collarbone had been smashed and two teeth knocked out and his testicles burnt with cigarette butts. Sweat broke out on his forehead and he turned back in the direction of Abdul's garage, panting with terror. Half a kilometre down the Katra road he stopped again and about-turned his trolley. And began slowly pedalling back the way he had come. He tried to think of the tall, calm man who did not take fright before a man in uniform but such courage was not for the likes of him, he knew. Still, there was another kind. Courage meant to be full of cowardly panic and to pedal with all one's might against the slope of one's fear, to scold down one's yammering imagination and pedal on, turn by turn of the wheel. If not the Commissioner's bungalow, where else could he carry this death-load? Where else if not Sankat Mochan Hanuman's deserted temple yard there at the end of the long cantonment road? For this was Lord Hanuman's city and he lay recumbent in his sunken sanctum in his riverside shrine, but smaller temples dedicated to him dotted the crossroads and along the mile-posts of the highways. A lonely highway-side temple with the vermilion god poised in stone against a pillar, brandishing his mace with one hand and lifting aloft a mountain with the other. Ah, Sankat Mochan knew what it was to bear a heavy weight, his own and all the world's, be it a whole mountain.

His trolley could easily be abandoned in the desolate temple yard. No one was there to notice, not a soul.

So in great and innocent simplicity of belief, Siddhu pedalled casually along the uneven brick pavement, parked his trolley at an angle to the sanctum, dismounted and made for the factory wall across the road. He pee-ed nonchalantly, finished, stood scratching his groin and then strolled to the paan shop some distance away and bought a bidi. He sauntered down the road to a guava stall and bought a guava, bit it and spat it out, calling the guava-wallah a cheat. He shambled some way further down the road, turned where the road swung in its most shaded curve and broke into a run. Right across the empty field he sprinted, over a mouldering wall and into the backyard of an old disused bungalow. No one in sight, the roof caved in, a rusted gate askew upon mildewed gateposts. Only a vast peepal tree with its massive branches outspread like the arms of a protective god. Siddhu threw himself down beneath its shade and sat shivering though the evening was hot. Hot flushes steamed his face and his temples pulsed.

'Hé Ram,' he thought. 'I did what I could, scared eunuch that I am.' Then a new thought struck him. Wouldn't the police find his fingerprints on the handlebars? And suppose some busybody came along and meddled with the cartons? Opened them and a crowd collected and helped themselves to free crackers! What if the paan-wallah and the guava-wallah remembered his face and the police made a sketch? In the lock-up they had threatened to castrate him with a sickle. Why had he made such a mess? 'Lord, ah Lord,' he sobbed, 'a feeble, craven worm am I! I can do big-big heroics and I can't even run away properly. My shivers follow me wherever I go. Lord, what a holy mess! A policeman's face can make me shit in my pants and now I've gone and gotten myself in trouble with the police again and they'll burn my balls and break my bones and belt my buttocks till I scream for death! Lord, what a fool, what a liverless wretch...' And so he babbled on and on and lost track of time.

It took him some time to see that the blurred world had not been created by his streaming eyes. Everything seemed to have been fogged over and the air was threaded with rain. Vapours rose from the cracked ground. Cool earth scents fumed. And he thought, 'Ah, Sankat Mochan has heard me. Rain!'

The realization rushed down his brain. The rain would erase his fingerprints! It would drench the soggy cartons, even soak past the protective plastic. If not the rain, the moist air would. It would reduce the entire consignment to damp squibs. 'Ah, Sankat Mochan,' he prayed. 'Let it pour. Let floods wash down and drown our heads like the surging Ganga does when we close our eyes and plunge into its whiteness.'

He had to avert his face from others at the bus stop, at the railway station and then in the general compartment of the train to Howrah. The train sped through vast, open country, from Allahabad to Mirzapur, to Mughalsarai, to Dehri-on-Sone, to Sasaram. Night fell. The downpour pounded its drumbeat on the roof of the train. Pebbly pellets of rain cantered against the windowpanes. Lightning sputtered, went teetering across a hairline crack of sky. Such a fireworks display up among the crashing clouds! Water got in through the slats of the shuttered windows, through cracks in doors and left baggage and footwear and the hem of women's sarees wet.

But is it raining back there? He wondered. He would never know. But when he awoke from a fitful drowse, sitting huddled against a fellow passenger some time of the night he saw that the train was standing at a small station. Somebody sprawled in the next berth was cursing into a mobile phone, 'Hullo, hullo, hullo! Hullo, hullo, to hell with this phone!' The voice explained to its invisible companion: 'This rain's upset all the signals from Dilli to Bihar. No signals at all.'

On his wooden berth Siddhu sat absolutely still. The signal had reached him, sure as a voice in his ear. He propped himself up and asked: 'Which station, Bhaiya?'

'Bodh Gaya,' said a man.

FOUR

Family Album

Triloki Singh wasn't like other slothful shop owners who lifted the shutters at eleven. He fretted when he was late and he was unusually late that day. He found that the petrol in his scooter had sunk to reserve and being the finicky man that he was, he parked the scooter at the wayside, walked to the nearest petrol pump, borrowed a five litre jerrycan to carry back the petrol, and after refilling, rode his scooter back to the petrol pump to return the jerrycan. A bad start to the day. And the ten-thirty traffic jam under the bridge near Niranjan Cinema—or what used to be Niranjan Cinema—had him beaten.

'You're so late today, Triloki-ji,' Vimla's voice called out from the store next to his.

'But still in time for chai.'

'These young sparks! Think the world is their baap-ki-jaidaad!' He blew into his tea. He was mad at his college-going son. 'Took my scooter to a shaadi. Used up nearly all the petrol. The whole family went to a shaadi—three of them piled up on a single scooter! How many times have I told them not to ride three to a scooter. But she, Renu, says—So why don't you buy us a Maruti instead?'

'You could, you know,' commented Vimla.

'Then everyone overslept this morning. No breakfast for me. Stale puris and sabzi for my lunch box! She, Renu, says—You should buy a fridge for your shop, ji. I said—It's a jewellery shop not a dhaba. Why should I buy a fridge for a jewellery shop? Then the girl giggles and says—You can use it as a locker for your special designs, Papa. Then they all laugh at me. Fridge by day for Papa's lunch, locker by night for Papa's baubles and gew-gaws!'

But Vimla said: 'Oh, never mind, Triloki-ji…in families we laugh at people we're fond of, not to be nasty, just friendly-like.'

'Much you know about it,' he grumbled. 'I told the boy to come and mind the shop for a couple of hours in the afternoon. He said—Sorry, Papa, got coaching in the afternoons. Asked the girl if she'd put in my letter to her Head of the Department. She said—Sorry, Papa, I forgot. This is the fourth time she's given me that answer. I'll go meet the Head of her Department myself today. I'll close the shop.'

'You don't have to, Triloki-ji. I'll mind your shop.'

He hesitated. 'How will you manage, Vimla-ji? You've got your own shop to mind.'

Her laugh was pitched somewhere between bitterness and self-deprecating good humour. 'It's not that customers are thronging in their hundreds to both our shops, Triloki-ji.'

He'd always marvelled at the calm way she said these things. 'You're sure?'

'Of course. Go and do your work. I'll manage. After all, your cash till and your receipt book are things I've handled before. I can't do your learned sales talk, though. All your talk about Mauryan girdles and Gupta hair pieces.'

'Oh, nothing to that. Just a few books I've read.' He brushed aside her compliment, the implication of superior education it suggested. Just a few books. He'd dropped out of college and taken over the shop when his father had the stroke that paralysed his right side. His father had dropped out too, for a quite different reason. Gandhi had sent round a call to students to boycott British Government-run institutions and his father, Trijugi Narayan Singh, had, with many other students, dropped out. Later he'd been very keen on his son getting a university education and his son had indeed joined the Allahabad University but, like a stubborn generation-spanning karma, things happened to make him drop out too. He had not gotten over the disappointment. Whenever dissatisfaction seized him, the vague, breathless disquiet that things had gone all wrong with him, his own threat or self-reassurance or subterfuge or solution was: I'll pick up my studies again. Then his son and daughter would go into fits of laughter. Papa and us in the same class, ha ha ha! Maybe we can help one another cheat in the exams, ha ha ha! Maybe we'll pass and Papa will plug, ha ha ha! He had an answer to that too—I'll join the Distance Education Course, and watch me then, young firecrackers, he said. But with time this dream had grown fuzzy about the edges. A course in what? Something to do with the history of jewellery. In what discipline would that fall? His present trip to the university was a vague shot in the dark.

He had a romantic idea of the university. He told the clerk in the office of the department he was visiting that he had an appointment with the Head. 'The Head was meeting a class,' the clerk told him. 'I shall take only two minutes of his time,' he assured the clerk. 'I'll see what I can do,' the clerk said. 'Go and wait outside the Head's chamber—he'll be there in a few minutes.' The Head was brusque. 'In two minutes time I have a Board of Studies meeting. If you are a guardian with a problem see the Dean Students' Welfare. If you are a research student's guardian, see the Deputy Registrar, Research Matters.'

'Sir, all I want is to ask you a question troubling me.' He produced a sketch out of his pocket. 'This stylized flower in the headgear of Mauryan women is exactly like the Lamura flower. Now the Lamura flower grows neither in India nor... nor in Macedonia or Greece or Persia. It is pentafoliate, with a distinctive thick calyx and is found in places in Northern Japan. So how to account for this...?'

The Head is in a hurry. He has never heard of the Lamura flower. I suggest you go to the General Library, he advises.

The usual guards at the gate of the General Library are missing. Triloki walks in, swinging his shoulder bag, without bothering about bag surrender, token or gate pass. He gets past the circular lobby. To the left he sees the Encyclopaedia Section which in a smaller font announces itself to be a Not-To-Be-Removed-Books Section. He steps in and is immediately caught up in the populous hush of timelessness that large libraries have. He moves from stack to stack, awed, diminished in his alienness to this world. He loses his sense of time though it is only a little over an hour.

Then he is hauled up by a library hand. 'You there with the bag! How did you manage to bring your bag in here?

May I see your gate pass? Your I-card?'

He is searched, his bag taken away and its contents examined. He is abashed, affronted but unfamiliar with the routine rituals of the university library. He is led into the Head Librarian's chamber. He expects the Head Librarian's chamber to be full of books but finds it bare and bureaucratic. There was no one at the gate, sir, he explains. Are you an employee? A teacher, a researcher? The Head Librarian is least bothered who or what he is, his manner suggests.

'I am a sort-of student, sir,' Triloki tries to explain his position. 'No, I am not a student of this university now though I was once, no, not an enrolled research scholar, no, I don't have an I-card, yes, I have a PAN card and a driving licence. I have a jeweller's shop and I am interested in ancient jewellery designs and I thought a library...I am interested in finding out about a stylized design of the Lamura flower which grows in Japan but is found in old Mauryan head pieces...'

The Head Librarian is a weary man. This isn't a library for the public, he tells Triloki, not unkindly. I suggest you go to the Public Library or better still the Museum.

There is no time to pack in another visit. He'd have to go to the Museum on another day. He rides his Bajaj scooter back to the store. To be met by an agitated Vimla.

'Any customers?'

'Oh, a most unusual one,' she says. 'She was, say twenty-ish. Quite a beauty, really. She asked to see some silver pieces. Anklets and arm-bands, not the usual things. And tikas and waist-key-bunches. She was very taken by a tika. And then she discovered she hadn't brought any money!'

'So what then?'

'So nothing. I said the proprietor is away—I'm just minding the shop for a while. Come again tomorrow, ma'am. She went away.'

He calculated the price of the large silver tika. A piece he'd crafted with loving precision, more as an adventure into the possibilities of his medium, the silver vines and whorls and whirligigs of foliage that even in the random flourish surprised themselves into unexpected rhythm. The gossamer filigree of silver trained into a mesh of such truant fibrillations that the thing exceeded the predictable and flowered into crazy, accidental symmetries. That's how he crafted his pieces. In old Delhi and Agra he'd sat with silversmiths, in Benaras and Kolkata with goldsmiths. He'd copied their ancestral motifs and improvised on them, much as a classical musician enclosed himself in the map of a raga's loose diagram and then sailed away far above it. That's how in his inarticulate way he'd worked out his private definition of freedom, to stay marginally tethered by a thread to the earth and then risk defying gravity as far as he could, testing the heights as far as they allowed, pushing his boundaries by design and craft. Design and craft. He thought of his work as artifices with his material, tricks on it and games with it. Not everyone liked his designs and most of his customers were curious foreigners exploring the lanes of the old city at Kumbha or Magh Mela time.

Next day the girl came again, a slender, tall, coltish thing with a restlessness in the eye and a simmering vibe in her movements. She had the strangest sloping gaze that tilted past the things they rested on into some whimsical reality of her own making. Her clothes were off-beat, her shoes maverick. She carried a kantha shoulder bag. She stepped softly, picking her way with fastidious grace like a ballerina about to float or swirl. Something secret and wary about each step as though she knew her feet were skilled in the art of transgressing into prized, forbidden places.

She came and stood in front of the counter and said nothing. Triloki waited for her to speak. When the moment began feeling too stretched he broke the silence.

'You're the lady who came yesterday?' He felt absurd calling this slip of a girl a 'lady'.

'Yes,' she said.

'Had you any particular piece in mind?'

'Yes,' she said again.

'Which one?'

She turned and scanned the glass cases which lined his walls with a perplexed look.

'That...that thing that hangs on your forehead...here.' She circled her forehead with a delicate finger.

'Ah, the tika,' he said.

'Yup,' she said.

He brought it out for her.

'Is there a mirror?' She looked around for one.

'Of course, madam.' She was young enough to be his daughter but he gave her the deference he would to a senior customer.

She tried to fix the tika in the parting of her hair. Failed. Tried and failed again. She uttered an exasperated gasp.

'If I may?' he offered. He managed to hitch it to her hair by the delicate silver hook but it slipped right off, sliding down the loose shining strand of hair and hanging askew at the side of her head.

'Just a minute,' he said. He nipped down to Vimla's shop to call her in to help.

Vimla took a hair-pin out of her own bun and fixed the tika on the girl's forehead expertly.

The girl frowned into the mirror he placed on the counter in front of her. Then suddenly she smiled. Tiny teeth, deep dimple, eyes all lit up.

'It suits me!' she cried.

'The wearer compliments the piece, madam,' he murmured one of his routine sales gallantries.

She turned her head left and right, surveying her face from all angles. Then she put her bag on the counter and drew out something tied in a large handkerchief.

'I haven't any money,' she said simply. 'So you'll have to take this.'

He was nonplussed. 'What?' The terms of the barter seemed bizarre.

She untied the handkerchief. An antique kundan choker. Gold. He was filled with panic.

'Ma'am. I couldn't,' he tried to reason with her.

'Why not?'

'It doesn't work this way.'

'Why not?'

'See—this is gold. What you want is silver. Your piece is worth several times the value of this tika.'

'No?' she said in childlike wonder.

It dawned on him that his misgivings are right. Something not quite right with her.

'I can't accept this,' he asserted firmly.

'Please,' she begged. Her eyes began filling.

'No, madam. If you like I can make you a pawn receipt for this gold choker and give you the money and deduct the price of the silver choker and you can come back later and redeem the gold item…'

She hadn't understood. 'Please,' she said with piercing intensity. A transformation was taking place before his eyes. Her face had kindled. There was a visible leap of manic energy into her pulsing pupils.

'Fuck all!' she hissed. Turned and stomped off, leaving her bag, her handkerchief, the gold choker flung upon his counter. He rushed after her but she was already at the end of the alley. He marvelled at her speed. He was at the end of his tether.

'Vimla-ji!' he called out in a strangled voice.

Vimla came. 'What now, Triloki-ji?'

'She's gone off. With the tika still on her head!'

It took Vimla time to make sense of it all.

'Run off with it, you mean? Ring up 100.'

'No, you don't get it. She's strange. Come in here and sit down.'

He showed her the clutter on the counter.

'She's even left her cell phone. Definitely a crazy one, Triloki-ji.'

'But what'm I to do now? See this gold piece.'

Vimla had picked up the cell phone. And was thoughtfully scrolling down. Her perplexed face had cleared. She showed him the contacts list. She had stopped at a particular number: PAPA. She pressed the button. After a couple of seconds she said, 'Hullo'. He could hear the voice at the other end. *Hullo*.

'Sir, I'm speaking from Trijugi Narayan, Triloki Chand

Khanna Jeweller's Company in the Chowk Bazaar. Your daughter has been here. We are waiting for you. Please come and collect your belongings.'

'What would I have done without your quick thinking, Vimla-ji?'

'It's nothing, Triloki-ji.'

Suspense built as they waited it out, nervously watching the end of the lane where it opened on to the main road. It was a quarter to six in the evening when a navy blue Swift Dzire drew up. He saw a stocky man, his own age, emerge from the driver's seat and from the seat alongside, the girl. He saw them walk towards his shop. The man scanned the shop signs, turned to ask directions from a fruit vendor. The girl was hanging back, dragging her feet. The man nudged her by the elbow. Even from a distance Triloki could see how firm that steering hand was on her skinny arm.

They entered the shop. Up close he saw a chain of silver hanging absurdly out of the breast pocket of the man's lawyer's coat like part of a military decoration. It had obviously been stuffed into the pocket in a burst of annoyance. Vimla stole in behind them.

The man did not look at Triloki. He talked to the girl.

'Where are your things?'

Silently Triloki produced them out of a drawer and placed them on the counter—the kantha bag, the cell phone, the gold choker and the handkerchief. The man picked up the choker.

'Ah, this one,' he said. He looked at Triloki for the first time. 'Are you sure there's nothing else?'

'No,' said Triloki.

'Are you sure?' asked the man. Triloki cursed him in his

heart. These bloody lawyers and their cross-questioning mode! Why would I have informed you about this if I meant to pinch it? thought Triloki, stung.

'Sure,' was all he said.

'Is this the only piece you gave this man in this…this absurd exchange?' the man asked his daughter. His manner of asking was—Is this man lying?

She nodded mutely. The man pulled out the silver tika and half tossed it on the counter.

'There,' he said. 'Yours, I understand.'

'Thank you,' said Triloki. A violent dislike for this man had flared in his head. He put the tika in its box, his face impassive. Began, from force of habit, to pack the choker in a fresh polythene case. His quiet method seemed to loosen something in the man standing across the counter. He lapsed into a fit of plaintive confidences.

'Think of my situation,' he pleaded. 'I couldn't leave the court when I got your wife's phone call…'

Both he and Vimla were embarrassed.

'Not my wife,' corrected Triloki, 'my…my…,' he faltered, confounded. What *was* Vimla to him? 'My good neighbour,' he finished, and Vimla, whose face had grown tense, visibly relaxed.

'I had three writs in a row and at the back of my mind this worry. If her mother was alive, there'd be someone to watch over her. As it is, the servants are terrified, especially when she is in these states. One thing after another and now this!'

'Has she no friends?' asked Vimla.

'She had some friends while she was going for her classes. But after she dropped out, they've stopped coming. After all, they're normal, focused kids with exams and careers ahead.'

Triloki felt like shouting at the man—'For God's sake, please! Stop discussing your daughter with strangers!' But he stood on the wrong side of the counter and years of programming had fostered the solicitude of meek agreement, the customer-is-always-right deference that was impossible to shake off. His blood boiled. He looked at the girl.

She seemed to have gone limp, her eyes inert, her posture slumped. She just wasn't there. They might have been discussing someone else.

He put the polythene-packed gold choker in the kantha embroidered bag, put in the cell phone. Then, on an impulse, he put the box with the silver tika in too. The girl's eyes followed his movements and sprang to life, startled.

'What are you doing?' asked her father.

He decided to ignore the man and spoke directly to the girl. 'For you, beta,' he said. 'You liked it, didn't you?'

The man sighed, felt for his wallet in his trouser pocket. His expression was weary. Trust a salesman to be a salesman, was what his face declared. 'How much?' he asked Triloki.

'Nothing,' said Triloki. 'She's already paid me.'

There was a minute's baffled silence, Triloki turned to the girl. 'Beta,' he said—he liked using that word for this demented child—beta, child, not 'madam', as he habitually used with female customers. 'Beta, I designed this piece in silver. You paid for it in gold. What more can I say? No one has paid me so much.'

The man flushed. Said something to the effect that he was needlessly pampering his daughter, turning her head. The girl's eyes widened, looked intently at him and went on looking.

Vimla stood quietly by. They saw the duo off.

When the Swift had driven off Vimla said softly, 'You're such an idealist, Triloki-ji. A real fool, but a good one.'

He waved her aside.

'It's nothing,' he said.

'You deserve a reward for this great and noble deed,' she said with teasing warmth.

'Tell me what I can do for you.'

'I have to go to the museum tomorrow. Please watch my shop for a couple of hours, Vimla-ji, will you?'

At the museum he deposits his jhola, takes out his sketch-pad and pencil and walks into the first hall to the right. He stops, spellbound at the sight that meets his eye, the massive space filled with opulent statuary, the floral friezes and lintels and door jambs, the jewelled arches, the piped, grooved, curlicued, looped, scalloped, arabesqued efflorescence. He begins sketching swiftly. He concentrates on the carved ornaments the figures wear and also the patterns in the stone meshwork, the screens, friezes, ribbed flutings.

There is a young man also studying the stone nayika whose girdle he is sketching. Suddenly as he plies his pencil on his page, he is startled by the flash of a camera. The young man moves on to the next mithuna figure, focuses his camera on the elaborate massed headgear. He is interested in that headgear himself. The flower-pin attached to the looped and clustered cascade knotted over the nape of the neck. He waits respectfully for the young foreigner to finish. Another flash. The mithuna figure stands bathed in lightning for a micro-second.

Then footsteps. A guard.

'Sir,' he approaches the young foreigner, 'no photography allowed inside hall.'

The foreigner turns to face the man.

'No photography, sir. Bad for stachoo.' This was a white man, hence the teeth-flashing deference. Triloki compared it to his own experience in the university library.

'Please to put away camera. If possible, please to deposit camera at gate counter.'

'Oh, okay,' said the young man. He went off, leaving Triloki sketching furiously.

'These goras,' jeers the guard, all complicity with his Indian compatriot now that the imperialist's descendant had left. 'Think they can do anything they please. I have heard you can't use camera in *their* museums, so does he think our museum is his baap-dada's jagir?'

'He didn't know,' said Triloki. 'Why didn't you search his bag, the way you searched mine?' Because he's white, because you feel you must flash your teeth? he thought, irritated. The guard turned away and Triloki turned to his sketch-pad, deftly copying the head-pin. He heard an intake of breath behind him and turned to see the foreigner looking over his shoulder.

'I say,' said the young man, 'look at that...' He indicated Triloki's sketch-pad.

Triloki looked, not latching on.

'I mean, that's great,' said the young man.

'Thank you,' said Triloki. 'I'm sorry you can't take your photos,' he said, just by way of polite conversation.

'Yeah,' said the other. 'Are there postcards of these figures... in the museum shop?'

'Only some.'

'But not from the angles I want...the kind of detail... like that there...' He pointed at the fine diamond-shaped meshwork of a nayika's gathered stole.

'True,' said Triloki. He saw the young man concentrating hard on the figure. A steadfast yet abstracted gaze as though he were committing the image to his visual memory and revising it again and again. He'd done it himself many times. He felt a strange kinship with this impassioned effort. An idea had just come to him.

He turned to the young man. 'If you like I can sketch it for you. I'll show you...' A few deft strokes and he had the figure, the thin netted gauze of its drape, the lissome curve of its languor down on paper. He tore out the sheet and passed it to his companion.

The stranger whistled. 'Brilliant!' he exclaimed.

After that first sketch Triloki did eight more, the two of them so absorbed that they didn't know when the clocks struck and when the closing-time siren sounded.

'Oh my God,' gasped Triloki. 'It's five and I forgot.'

'What?' asked the young man.

'My shop. I left a friend to mind it...and I forgot all about it.'

His companion was sympathetic. 'Sorry,' he said. 'It's my fault.'

Triloki would have none of it. 'Nonsense,' he said. Then it occurred to him that he didn't know this stranger's name. 'Mr...?' he asked.

'Jameson,' said his new friend. 'Jamie to you.'

Triloki knew a few things about textbook history. 'You

are British,' he deduced.

'Right.'

'English people had kings called James. The Scottish did too,' expounded Triloki in all seriousness. 'James the sixth of Scotland became James the first of England.'

The young man's lips twitched. 'That so? I'm Scottish,' he added. 'No relation though.'

'No?' responded Triloki, still serious. 'Mr James,' he said, 'You are a guest in my country. I see you are an artist.'

'I'm a photographer. How about you?'

'I'm a jeweller,' said Triloki.

'How interesting! A designer or a retailer?'

'I design,' said Triloki bashfully.

'Uh hunh,' breathed Jameson, 'I'd be interested in seeing your work then.'

'Really?'

'Very much indeed. Let me take down your phone number.'

Triloki dictated it to him. 'I'll also give you the address of my showroom.' He scribbled it on the back of a sketch.

'Great! See you then.'

'See you,' said Triloki.

Back at the shop Vimla is ready with the afternoon's highlights.

'She's been here—that girl. Her name is Naina.'

Alarm bells in Triloki's head.

'Don't look so panicky, Triloki-ji. She's quite harmless. Quite a child really. She came to my shop and looked through my designs. She loves trying them on in the trial room. And she laughs and claps her hands when something looks good on her. Most of it does—she's such a little beauty.'

'Lots of work for you, Vimla-ji.'

'Not a bit, Triloki-ji. When there are no customers it's good to have someone trying on your things—even if she isn't buying. I don't mind the folding up at all. In fact it's good to see someone actually wear them.'

'You're a nice woman, Vimla,' was what he wanted to say but didn't.

Back home his wife asks if he's sold anything recently. He tells her about the tika, the girl, the British man at the museum.

'You mean you just gave it away?' She is incensed.

He bristles. 'Yes,' he says, defiant.

'Why? Is she young? Is she pretty?'

'Forgodssake—she's about as old as our daughter.'

'More reason then. No fool like an old fool.Oh, you men!'

He is enormously irritated but goes on eating.

'Nita,' he asks when his daughter enters. 'Did you give my letter to your Department Head?' Just to test her. Just to prove something to himself.

'Sorry, Papa, I lost it. Please don't be mad. Give me another one—I'll give it tomorrow.'

There. Exactly as he'd thought.

'Papa,' said his son. 'Can I borrow your scooter?'

He hummed in resigned assent.

'And Papa. Money for petrol.' He reached for his wallet.

In the shop next day the girl appeared. She flopped down on a modha in Vimla's showroom and watched Vimla work.

'Chai?' asked Vimla.

'Triloki-ji. Naina Bitiya is here!' Vimla called.

Naina Bitiya put on a bridal lehnga in phalsahi pink, then

came into his jewellery store and pointed at a pair of massive earrings in his showcase. He took them out—helped her on, gave her the mirror and shared in her tinkling laughter.

'Now try this one,' he says, taking out another choice piece.

She runs into Vimla's store, rushes into the trial room, appears a few moments later in a mustard sharara, with Vimla in tow.

'How nice that mustard thing looks on her,' said Vimla. 'I had no idea it would look this good.'

The name of the game was doll dressing. 'Gudiya-gudiya,' as Vimla later called it. Then as the girl is posing in a mauve anarkali churidar-suit, Jamie turns up.

'I say,' he says. 'That's drop-dead stunning. Just hold it.' He takes out his camera and clicks. Shows them the image. They are astonished. She stands, one foot stork-straight, the other resting on the tips of her toes in a moment just short of a dance flight, the gathers round the ankles piled up in fine chiselled circlets of silk. The fitted bodice of the sequined anarkali kurta hugged her form and the skirt belled out in full drapes to halfway down the calf. The matching net odhni climbed her head in a crowning affectation, framing her face in intricate rice-pearl scallops, and swung back in languid coquetry over the right shoulder, the left trailing its misty transparency down the front panels of her dress.

Naina looked hard at her image in Jamie's camera and began laughing joyfully. They exclaimed over it by turns. Naina bounded to Vimla's showcase, took out a dress on a hanger and rushed for the trial room. She emerged dressed in it, struck a pose and looked round for applause.

'What's that costume called?' Jamie wanted to know.

'That's a peshwaz. A nineteenth century fashion,' said Vimla.

'Those crusted stonework borders are marvellous. You really did it yourself?'

Vimla nodded.

'Where did you learn such embroidery?'

Vimla hesitated. 'We learnt it in my family. My ancestors have been doing it for hundreds of years. They were Jadias from Rajasthan and they settled in this city in Akbar Badshah's time.'

Jamie clicked a couple more shots. 'Know what? This deserves some strong gold enhancement,' he remarked.

'You're right,' agreed Triloki. 'And I know just the piece to go with it.'

He fetched it, taking care to lock up after, also taking care to stand on Vimla's steps so as to keep an eye on his own shop.

Vimla helped Naina on with the massive pushpahar, the large jhumar down the side of the head and the ratna-choor on the hand.

'What's that?' asked Jamie.

'That's an ornament for the hand. It's called a ratna-choor. It's a bracelet connected with five floral gold chains to five rings, one for each finger.'

Naina fluttered her hand round her veil and Jamie clicked.

'There's something called a charan-choor too. For the foot.'

'You guys are just amazing,' said Jamie. 'How many ensembles have you created?' he asked Vimla.

'In my sketchbook, maybe two hundred. On the shelves maybe—let me see, seventy or so at the moment.'

He whistled. 'And how about you?' he asked Triloki.

'Oh, I don't know. I haven't counted. Yes, at the rate of ten designs or so every six months for about twenty-two years...'

'Can I see your designs?'

'Oh, why not?'

They are most flattered. Sitting there on the steps, Jamie pores over their two sketchbooks.

'You know what—you guys should be in all the big-time fashion magazines. With downtown stores in metros. With supermodels on ramps and actresses as show-stoppers...'

Triloki and Vimla start laughing.

'What are you laughing at?'

'All that's your fantasy, not ours,' says Vimla. 'We rarely sell a couple of items each week—and that's a record.'

'Listen, you've got to listen. You've got to advertise. You get me? Advertise.'

'Costs money.'

'You've got to show people what you can do. Take your work to the world.'

'Where is the world?' smiles Triloki. 'This is Ram Narain Ki Bagiya lane. This is our world.'

'Look,' says Jamie, 'if you aren't able to access the world, make sure the world accesses you. The world is here—at your doorstep. The Kumbha Mela, you dumbos. That's what I'm here for. I'm a photographer for *The International* and I'm covering the Kumbha.'

Triloki was impressed though he'd never heard of *The International*. It sounded like the name of a hotel but was probably a news magazine.

'So how do we get the Kumbha to advertise us? Shall we design for the Babas and the hippies? Shall we set up a memsahib lady-Baba to preach to the pilgrims about us?' Triloki sniggered, finding this idea funny beyond words.

'For a pair of gifted artists you really are slow,' scolded Jamie. 'I mean, it's a great pity, look at you. It's just a week short of the Paush Purnima and then this Kumbha Mela goes on till Shiv Ratri—that's mid-March this year. How many people come? Check the statistics. Five crores expected, my travel agent tells me. Your target market isn't pilgrims but the celebs, the photographers, the journalists, the models and film stars and the wives and girlfriends of politicians and tech-millionaires. What you need is hand-outs. Brochures. Flyers. You've got the loveliest model here. And I'll be your photographer. All you do is roll up the sleeves and plunge into work. We'll do it, man.'

The idea grows on them. A CD with twenty-five designs. A brochure with five. And a flyer. Work out the cost. How many? Say, a thousand. A thousand! You must be joking. You've got to accept this—anything less than a thousand isn't worth it. Who'll we give them to? Believe you me, you'll fall short. The paper has got to be classy. CDs cost ten bucks each. Thirty thousand at a rough estimate. Triloki is not convinced. We'll never recover that, he jitters. But Jamie thinks otherwise. Of course you will. Think of the orders you'll get. The publicity. Triloki's wife absolutely forbids his investing fifteen thousand rupees. Vimla contributes her share of fifteen. Triloki tries persuading his wife so she invites them all to dinner so as to assess the venture. The evening is a disaster. Triloki's son asks Jamie to sell him his jeans. 'What?' Jamie roars with laughter. 'D'you expect me to go home wearing *that*?' Jamie points at the boy's terrycot trousers. Triloki's daughter is having the sulks. Why can't I be a model too? her eyes accuse Triloki, who ignores them. Triloki's wife takes a dislike to both Jamie and Naina and has only contempt for Vimla. She put her foot down. 'The girl is mad, the foreigner is a sharp one,' she tells Triloki later. 'How much is he expecting to make out of you, say?' she demands to know. 'Those angrezes made a colossal lot of money out of us, everyone knows. As for that Vimla, what she needs is a man, or didn't you guess?'

'Oh, shut up, woman,' thunders Triloki and storms out of the room. He arranges to borrow fifteen thousand from a broker he knows by pawning one of his gold pieces.

The thing picks up. 'We'll do location shoots,' decides Jamie. 'Outdoors, since indoor shoots involve permission, etc. And delays. Let's make a list of sites. Which clothes will go with the natural colours of the site—complement it or underscore it? Where to get the best effects? Company Bagh greenery—' 'Sorry, it's called Chandra Shekhar Azad Park,' Triloki coughed gently. 'Whatever. Against the Victoria monument the marble and green will be a fantastic backdrop for that magenta ensemble and if you pair it with silver jewellery...'

'I haven't any proper shoes,' said Naina surprisingly.

'Never mind. Barefeet is the style. Henna your feet,' said Jamie.

'Not to forget the charan-choors,' put in Triloki.

'Where else? A boat on the Yamuna at the break of dawn. That'll majorly support the texture of that salmon pink and cloud-grey outfit.'

'The moonstone jhoomar!' exclaimed Triloki.

'Exactly.'

And so it went. Jamie and Triloki visited Saraswati Offset in Katra Bazaar and discussed the brochure. They went to Muthigunj to find the best paper and buy it in bulk.

'What about my make-up?' wondered Naina.

'I'll ask my friend Savitri who runs a beauty parlour.'

'No, it'll have to be done on-site. We've got two weeks to do it in. That's roughly three shoots a day. You can't manage three trips to the beautician and also count on the light staying right.'

'We can organize it in such a way that the heavy ensembles have professionally done make-up and the lighter ones we can trust to our own skills...'

'And what beautician will be available at five-thirty in the morning when we do the sunrise-on-the-Yamuna shots?' scoffed Triloki.

'Stop being such a spoilsport, Triloki-ji. If I ask my beautician friend—and maybe create a dress specially for her—she will come. Only, she'd naturally like her name and the name of her beauty parlour mentioned on our brochure.'

'That's fair enough,' said Jamie. 'But I hope she knows her job. Naina here looks like a million dollars without any make-up and the make-up lady had better know how to do this face that'll one day launch a million cameras!'

Naina laughed, flung herself on him and hugged him. Triloki could've sworn that was the moment that special vibe began, that something-in-the-air like jasmine itr overhanging the senses. The lilt in Naina's voice, the warm shine in Jamie's eyes.

The CDs were done, so were the brochures. They gathered in Triloki's shop to share in the excitement of unpacking the parcels, of viewing the CD on Jamie's laptop. Over chai and a plateful of Hari samosas they discussed the individual images, how they'd managed a particular effect, how something could have been better or how some accidental factor had worked in their favour.

After the brochures and CDs were ready there came the matter of packaging. There was no possibility of a stall. They weren't registered. Besides, pointed out Triloki, they weren't selling anything, just handing things out for free.

'Still those policemen and their haftas,' worried Vimla.

'We can keep changing sites. After all, the Kumbha mela sprawls across acres and acres as far as the eye can see. So we can keep turning up at different spots each day.'

'That'll mean being mobile. Having some sort of vehicle,' mused Jamie.

'Well, how about hiring a taxi and putting up a display on its hood?'

'Too expensive,' murmured Triloki.

'Papa's away,' offered Naina suddenly. 'For fifteen days. I can bring our car.'

'You'll drive it, Princess?' Jamie wanted to know.

'Sure, I will.'

'Hey,' exclaimed Jamie, 'how'bout adding a bit of drama to the proceedings? Add more zing, fun. Princess here all dressed up in one of these fancy royalty togs, drives up, parks. Liveried attendant jumps out. Me. Unrolls a red rug, holds up a parasol. Princess steps out and receives his deep salaam. Just a two minute act in costume. With music playing in the car...'

'Why would the princess be driving? Wouldn't she have a chauffeur?'

'I can be the liveried chauffeur then.'

The fun of it was catching. Why not a flower-decked rickshaw? Why not a decked-up sabzi-cart with a garden umbrella on it? Why not a country boat moored to the Nehru Ghat bank? Why not a baraat horse with Princess and me on it? Why not a Ram Lila chowki with all of us in it, all decked out in period costume?

'Please, please!' Triloki had to shout to be heard. 'We're all going over the top. Let's be practical. We can only go for things that don't cost a pile. Okay, the car and the sabzi cart and the rickshaw are fine but the horse and the boat...'

'Yup. Right you are. Maybe the horse'll poo and it'll come down like a mountain of smoking mud all over the place and then?'

'Oh, we'll turn it into a skit and call it *The Princess And the Poo*,' guffawed Jamie and reached out for her hand.

'No, seriously, some of those ideas sound good but there will be those special bathing days when vehicles aren't allowed in without a pass, so forget your rickshaws and thelas and horsy ideas.'

'On those days we'll carry the stuff in backpacks and be the display ourselves,' said Jamie.

'How?'

'Oh, wear coordinated clothes, have elaborate turbans on our heads.'

'Come on, you'll be suggesting we carry harmoniums tied round our necks and tom-toms too.'

'Why not put a tom-tom on a bike. Better, on your scooter, Triloki-ji.'

'Don't be asinine, Vimla-ji.'

They were all a little tipsy with the thrill of this thing, all chattering and leg-pulling, all high.

Then Triloki had a hugely sobering thought.

'Who's to mind our shops? I mean, if customers come pouring in and find the shutters down? What's the sense of all this then?'

'True,' agreed Vimla. 'In the fun of it we've forgotten the sales angle.'

'Life's about fun more than sales,' pronounced Naina sagely.

'For you, ma'am,' commented Vimla. 'You who can exchange gold for silver!'

They roared with laughter, remembering. Naina loudest.

'No, but someone's got to mind the shops,' fretted Triloki, helping himself to another samosa.

'You could request Bhabhiji,' said Vimla hesitantly. 'And maybe your kids.'

'Not they,' said Triloki gloomily. 'Can't be sure about them.'

'But there's no one else really,' he thought aloud. 'That's the thing. No one else apart from these people that fate and biology have given us, and fate plus biology plus obligation adds up to what?—The Great Indian Family! Let me approach my great Indian family then,' a wave of bitterness swept over him. They're all we have.

His wife was nasty about it, as he'd expected.

'So you go gadding about and I'm left holding the baby!'

'You're left minding the hearth and the cash-till,' he explained patiently. 'Those are the most important things. The reason we've taken on this huge exercise.'

In his heart he knew there was one more reason. The

sheer joy of this novel undertaking. The heady engagement of it. His wife agreed, with his sulky son and daughter also volunteering to do shifts. Vimla arranged for her sisters to take time off from their jobs and sit in her shop by turns.

Eventually it amounted to those ideas—the car with music playing, the Princess alighting, the marigold-decked rickshaw, the sabzi-cart with the garden umbrella, the backpacks and turbans on Makar Sankranti and Mauni Amavasya days. Jamie combined it all ingeniously with his photography assignment of the Kumbha Mela, its crowds of plodding pilgrims, its ash-smeared, chillum-smoking ascetics, its hordes of foreigners in floral cheesecloth skirts, their hair in dreadlocks, and beads and chains round their necks. Its huge pandemonium and trumpeting processions. Its elephants crowned with silver howdas holding the senior echelons of the various orders of the Hindu monastic hierarchies. Its acres of stalls and millions of people-milling, jostling crowds wearing every conceivable Indian costume, speaking every conceivable language. In the middle of all this swirling energy, their own little quirky skit, crazy, over the top, but thrilling. Every moment of it.

They handed out their CDs, taped to their five-page brochure. And were surprised when many clamouring hands reached out to take them. The most unlikely of people. Women constables, shivering pilgrim ladies, bureaucrats in their blue-beacon Ambassador cars driving past, the plump wives of judges of the High Court. Tall, grey-eyed foreign women with flaxen hair and lined faces, bearded kurta-and jean-clad all-weather, all-subject discussants, brainstormers in cargoes and jackets and motivational guru types in pin-striped shirts and trousers and designer winter-wear. It got pretty chaotic on occasion and left their tempers frayed.

'Don't hand it to those who won't ever buy,' hissed Triloki.

'How do I know if they'll buy or not? Is it written on their faces?' hissed back Vimla.

'There are many who definitely can't read,' observed Triloki.

'So what are the pictures for?' demanded Naina.

'I mean, if you can't afford an education, you probably can't afford to indulge in a dress like this,' Vimla pointed out.

'Ah,' reacted Triloki, cut to the quick. Education was his bete noir, his rawest nerve.

She saw her mistake, laid a hand on his arm.

'Not that way, Triloki-ji,' she implored in a small voice.

He shook off her arm.

'It's alright,' he said gruffly.

A raucous voice issued forth from the massive loudspeaker fitted on its tall pole right behind them: Wake up! Wake up, O my soul! For this world is illusory and all your attachments ephemeral too. Aeons shall pass and millions of lifetimes without a glimpse of those you cherish so!

By fortuitous circumstance when it drizzled on Mauni Amavasya day they had a large garden umbrella to huddle under. They'd carried it, two by two, on foot because on this most important bathing day vehicles weren't allowed into the sacred area of the mela. Holding it upright at times to get through the queues. By the same fortuitous circumstance they found themselves in the company of Katherine Russel one day, then Shivani Munshi and Shivraj Munshi and even that ultimate icon of the great Indian masses, Amitabh Bachchan. Katherine Russel was here, looking for meaning and peace, after her recent split with her rockstar partner. Shivani and

Shivraj were religious and loved getting photographed by hand-picked camera-men as they bowed before shrines, laid sheets on tombs or took dips in holy streams. The ultimate icon seemed to be there only to add to the agitation of the cops and the crowds, offering competition to the river as the star attraction of the mela. The Prime Minister had come and gone, and so had the Chief Minister. Their helicopters had hovered in the sky like giddy dragonflies and turned into a speck in the clouds and vanished. There remained a hush-hush list of world figures who kept their arrivals and departures an internationally guarded secret for reasons of privacy and security.

'See what I meant?' said Jamie. 'The world has come calling at your door. You're massively connected, man. You're almost there!'

Triloki nodded, unable to speak for the excitement, the noise, the happy exhaustion.

'So?' asked his wife when he returned home. 'How did it go?'

'Good enough,' he answered in his most maddeningly non-committal voice. Sometimes, for an incomprehensible reason, he loved thwarting her curiosity, enjoyed the frustration in her face with avenging joy.

'How many?' she pursued.

'Enough,' he said. Then he checked himself. He had questions of his own that he'd forgotten.

'Any customers?' he asked with guileful innocence.

'Not enough,' she said in a deadpan voice that he recognized as *her* corresponding combat mode.

'How many exactly?' he asked, reduced to meekness.

She noticed the micro-shift in his stance and would have none of it.

'Hardly any,' she replied.

'Ten, twelve, fifteen?' he asked.

She seemed to derive some satisfaction in the answer she gave, like a conclusive trump.

'Just two.' Then taking pity on him, she relaxed, let go. 'Both foreigners,' she added.

'Ah!' there seemed little else to say.

'You didn't tell me, ji, how you raised the money,' she said.

'You didn't ask,' he replied.

'I waited for you to tell me.'

'I waited for you to ask.'

That's how it was between them. Subtle accusations, obliquities, reproachful circularities. It had become a test of resilience for both, a ball-game that neither won. But she continued to sit in the shop and continued to hector his son and daughter to put in their shifts and for that he was grateful. But he didn't show it and knew he never would.

By mid-February the mela had ebbed like the receding waters of the rivers in summer. The last important bathing day, Vasant Panchami, fell on the 14th of February.

'Valentine's Day!' exclaimed Naina and half turned to Jamie with a soft, expectant smile.

'It's our Spring Festival,' explained Triloki. 'For us, Allahabadis, it is the day *we* go to take our dip. The other bathing days, Paush Purnima, Makar Sankranti, Mauni Amavasya, we leave to our pilgrim guests and visitors. But Vasant Panchami is *our* day.'

'So it should,' said Jamie enthusiastically. 'But by now, am

I a visitor or a local, I wonder.'

'To us you're a local.'

'Then let's go take our dip!' said Naina.

'How? Where do we leave all this stuff of ours?'

Triloki, in the simplicity or stupidity of his heart, suggested that the two women go first and the two men later, but Jamie artfully side-stepped that one, took Naina by the arm before Triloki could come forward and said, 'See you then.'

He saw the two of them vanish in the river-front crowd incredulously, then in slow comprehension, turned to stare at Vimla and raised his eyebrows in questioning.

'Exactly as you think, Triloki-ji,' she confirmed. 'It's Valentine's Day that the young people are going crazy about these days. The day birds begin building nests and singing to charm their mates.' She spoke in wistfulness, she who'd built no nest, just grown old looking after younger sisters and old mother, just kept an old nest from disintegrating.

Triloki laughed sceptically. 'If you mean those two, what nest? He's an angrez. She's cute but not all there. He might be married. She might not leave that strict father of hers. And what does she know of him?'

'Oh stop, stop, Triloki-ji. Must you think so far? See, the mela will start dismantling tomorrow. The tent-city, the shops, these huge pavilions, everything. Like it does every year. People go away and return for the next one. The annual Magh or the Ardha Kumbha or the Big Kumbha after twelve years. Where we're standing the river shall be flowing during the monsoons. Sometimes those very same people don't come back. But others do in their place. And they do the same things. Oh, I can't put it clearly—don't you understand?'

He could. She was saying it didn't matter who came, who went, who loved, who separated. The thing was that a city had come into being, like a giant nest, and now its season was coming to an end, but the thing would happen again and other temporary, tenuous unions might happen and then unhappen. Not just this Kumbha-Nagari, poised one final night on the edge of quiet dismantling but the month-long spell they'd all inhabited, the charged bonding, the compulsive energy of creating something together. He wasn't a man of articulate thought but the full weight of what they'd all shared rested on his mind. Like pilgrims taking a dip, the thought flitted through his head.

When Jamie and Naina returnd, soaked through and laughing, the sight of their radiance, the shine of their sanded limbs, their streaked, wet hair, was like a wash in the Ganga for Triloki.

'Now your turn to take that dip,' said Jamie.

But Triloki said, 'No, I've had my dip.'

And Vimla, always sensitive to his switches of mood, said no too. 'I haven't got a change of clothes and I'm prone to chills. Not young like the two of you,' she said.

The fact was that this pairing was getting too much. The fact was that it had to be thus far and no further. There were risks one might take at twenty-five that one might not be willing to take at fifty.

'Oh, at least go and put some Ganga water on your heads,' said Naina.

Triloki could see she wanted to be alone with Jamie a little bit more. So, more in consideration of her wishes, Vimla and he went, gruff, not looking at one another. She lifted two palmfuls of water and drank it, eyes closed and an old remembered mantra on her lips. He watched her drink deep, as though she was very, very thirsty. On an impulse he bent and lifted two palmfuls of water and overturned it in the parting of her hair. She jerked up, spluttering, her eyes smarting, glaring at him.

'What're you doing, Triloki-ji?' she snapped.

'Just waking you up,' he said.

'Then let me do the same,' she said playfully, and before he knew what she was about, she'd poured two handfuls of Ganga water on his head.

'That's enough, Vimla-ji,' he scolded, cross. 'I'm awake now and so are you.'

'Now let's go and wake those two up. It'll be a lot harder,' she said soberly.

Jamie flew back in the third week of February. Naina's father returned and made her fill out entrance exam forms for a number of courses in Delhi colleges, Bangalore colleges and Pune colleges. In all fifteen outfits and six sets of jewellery were sold. The thirty thousand was not recovered in full. In fact a big deficit. About a hundred brochures and CDs remained with them.

'Maybe I can keep some?' asked Naina. 'Papa thinks I am going to study law and work in some lousy law firm but I know what I'm going to do. I'm going to get into modelling and thanks to you guys I even have a portfolio now.'

'You can have as many as you like, bitiya,' said Triloki. 'May it bring you lots of offers.'

'One day,' said Naina, 'I'm going to be a supermodel and then you both will be my designers.'

'Ghee and sugar in your mouth, girl,' laughed Vimla. 'Triloki-ji, may I keep a few too? My beautician friend asked for some. Maybe we can do a dress-lending business combined with a party make-up line. These brochures might come in useful.'

'Oh, go ahead and take all you want,' said Triloki. He'd heard of Vimla's new business idea but didn't want to join it. Jewellery shouldn't be lent out too freely, especially original designs—it cheapened the inspiration that created it. He was fanatical about this. 'Just leave a couple for me and take the rest,' he told them.

It was their last afternoon together. Sitting at the Netram stall in the residual Kumbh mela, lunching on halwai-made kachowries, aaloo-zeera, sour pumpkin sabzi, raita and tamarind-jaggery chutney with Jamie taking photographs all through the meal.

'Maybe we'll all come together next Kumbha,' said Naina.

'Why not? We just might,' agreed Jamie.

Next Kumbha. Twelve years in the future.

'How old will you be twelve years from now?' Triloki asked Jamie.

'Let me see. I'm thirty-two—so I'll be forty-four. Hooh! Proper middle-aged!' he rolled his eyes despairingly.

'And I'll be thirty-two then,' squealed Naina. 'Omigod, all wrinkled and grey!' She pulled a face.

Vimla laughed and laughed. 'Oh you stupids!' she exclaimed, 'You idiots! I'll be sixty in twelve years' time and watch me!'

Triloki scanned the large expanse of the river flowing ahead of him, the broad moving sheet of it, the mist-shrouded bank on the far side.

'I'll be sixty-four,' he sighed, adding up the years.

'But why just a couple of brochures for you, Triloki-ji?' Vimla wanted to know. 'Don't you have any plans for them yourself?'

'No,' he answered. 'I'll keep one to look at and one in reserve. In case the first one gets lost.'

'Look at?'

'Like one looks through an album,' he explained. 'A family album.'

FIVE

The Paan-woman of Khusrau Bagh

Some say she came from Istanbul. Others that she was a local. Nothing is known of her. That extra monument, mysteriously known as the Tamolan's Tomb, stands in the Khusrau Bagh, guarding its secret.

*N*obody could have believed they were not what they pretended to be. They sat begging, heads shaved to bristly, stubbled scalps, their rough, ragged length of cotton cowled over their bowed heads and around their scrawny bodies. Benaras widows they had made themselves. They begged in frayed voices beside the ghats. They told their beads at the Bade Ganeshji Temple. They helped to make garlands at the Kashi Vishvanath Temple. Benaras widows was what they became for a dozen years and might have remained till the end of their days had Raushni not come to regard the sight of the cremations at the Manikarnika Ghat with such terror. 'One day,' she took to saying more and more frequently, 'I shall go back to my father, the Khan-e-Azam, Mirza Aziz

Koka, and be buried in a grave and await the day of Allah, but what will you do without me, my Yamuni?'

'Never mind me, my lady,' is what Yamuni used to tell her, 'I might turn into a paan-wali again, a tamolan, and don't forget…Benaras is the city for paans.'

The mention of paan made a quietness fill their eyes and a little coil of pain tighten in their throats. From a chattering tamolan of Agra's Meena Bazaar to a Dashashwamedh widow, who could have said? They had spent so many years alongside one another, in grief and panic that they often found themselves thinking identical thoughts, visioning parallel memories. An acute pang of loss stirred piercingly in their brains as the image of him arose as he looked that day when he plucked the pearl-tipped silver pin from the dainty silver-foiled bida of paan, smiled and tucked it in his kimkhwab choga front, saying, 'For sure I must be careful, ladies, lest this pierce my delicate heart that lies beneath!' He could be a charmer, that one, and in the prime of his early days in court, a refined flirt. Great soldier he could be in the field of battle, an irresistible wit in the Emperor's durbar chamber, could turn an elegant verse to a fellow courtier and was a proven star among lovers in the harem. The bida of paan he had beckoned her for and she had, with trembling hands, lifted it to his handsome lips and hesitated a palm's width away until he had gently taken hold of her wrist. The manner of his accepting the paan was such you might have thought it was just an excuse for kissing a maiden's proffered hand.

Even after two score years she could see him in her mind's eye, reclining against two piled-up velvet bolsters, his lustrous hair free of the brocade headgear now laid beside him on the low brocaded takht, wisps of hair a-stir to the rhythm of the fan-women's movements. His aristocratic beard sleek upon the cautious working jaw that paused upon the tender paan as he tested the flavours that loosed their palette of aromas upon his tongue.

'I have, by Allah, never tasted this thing before,' was what he said, 'but this I will grant you, the Malika-e-Hind for once knows what's good for the mulk.'

For it was she, the Malika-e-Hind, Nur Jahan, Empress of India and strategist par excellence, who'd started this fashion of paan-chewing in the Mughal court. Paan had been a fragrant relish of our land, a cure for many ills, and a history as long as the ancient books of our Hindu vaidyas and kavirajas, as old as the sinuous carvings of lovers on our temple panels who locked their lips together over a shared twist of paan. But the Malika-e-Hind, that most beauteous of queenly strategists who well knew that to cast a spell on an Emperor, besotted as much with drink and opium and the tempests of his unsteady brain as with the beauty and wit of this temptress tactician of a lady wife, all methods, those known to statecraft and those which were whispered secrets of the harem, were valid and welcome. She it was who'd discovered the effect of ripe, luscious lips reddened with paan on the pulse-beats of men and she it was who'd started the fashion, first among the women of the harem and the ladies-in-waiting and the wives of the nobility and gentry, and the fad had caught the fancy of the men as well. With the result that chains of betel stalls now dotted the bazaars and squares and alleys. Silversmiths fashioned ornate betel boxes with compartments to hold the ingredients and customize individual flavours to suit individual tastes and little boxlets shaped like books to hold just a couple of bidas, small enough to fit tunic pockets, and betel-pins with tiny beads and sharp points to spear the cone in place, and delightfully graceful spittoons to receive the jet of scarlet juice that fountained forth from courtly mouths. Courtesans perfected the ceremonies of the grace of offering paan and saucy paanwalis like herself, honed the skills of repartee and riposte for which they became famous.

Much after moon-rise it was that time, the musicians serenading the Kartik night with the zephyrs of an evening raga that blew around the lofty vaults and cornices and silk hung alcoves like the first breath of incoming winter. He had partaken of his dinner and unlike his father and all his princeling step brothers, he was sober as a scholar. Which, as everyone knew, he was. He had eaten his portion of yawlma, which you must know was an elaborate Mughal preparation that had kept the master artists of the palace bawarchikhanas intensively engaged, scolding and swearing at their minions and underlings, until the entire ensemble was impeccably stood up on its massive gold platter. A whole goat, stuffed with exotic spicemanship and the artifice of generations of grandmasters of the royal kitchens. It had taken four minions to be the festive litter-bearers of this ornately bedecked beast, and they'd hastily pulled on their silver-cloth tunics and scarlet cummerbunds with the perky panaches before carrying it with choreographed steps to the dastarkhwan chamber of her ladyship, the Princess Ain-e-Raushnaq, senior-most wife of Sultan Mirza Khusrau. Khusrau, it was widely known, loved his yawlma with kamrakh chutney, a tart, tangy dip which was, to begin with, Prince Khurram's favourite but had now found favour with scores of palace princelings quite as the betel leaf had.

'Tell me,' he'd addressed her, 'how you create this witchery.'

She had bowed low, made obeisance, and stammered, all flushed and confounded in being thus singled out for attention: 'Sire, by your leave we use the tenderest leaves. We fill fine-chopped dry areca nut on the upper left half and fine-chopped tender areca nut on the upper right—thus. The pouch created, my lord, we fill as it suits the choice—with tobacco and lime and the extract of the acacia tree. Or for gentler palates with cloves or candied rose petals. With fennel seeds, coconut and cardamom, with mint or camphor...'

He had started laughing fondly at the nervous gravity with which she delivered the procedure.

'Enough, girl,' he stopped her. 'We stand converted to this kufr. And when perchance I am Sultan of Hind and beseated on the takht of Empire we shall build a Pavilion to the Paan and get Vilas Khan to compose a Paanraga and sing panegyrics to it. When I am Emperor and some scribe happens to write a Khusraunama....'

Here the Princess Ain-e-Raushnaq, who had all this while gazed on her man with soft doting eyes, hastily laid a hand upon his sleeve and said, 'Hush, my lord, rein in this rash talk.'

No Khusraunama was ever written for, as it transpired, he did not rein in, neither his talk of kingship nor his active preparations. On the streets and squares his name was lauded, a soldier par excellence, a being of sharp intelligence, sane as his father Jahangir was not, with his flailing mood swings, his long sodden absences from sense. In the chambers and halls of office in the Fort his credit was high, with factions backing his cause and loyalists ready to do battle under his standard. It could not have been safe for him, with whispering spies everywhere, those in Nur Jahan's secret employ, those in his step-brothers', those in his father's, too many stealthy self-seekers who would rob their mother's shroud for a piece of gold. But with all his gifts, with his clarity of mind and his high-minded principles of statecraft, our prince placed too much faith in that most traitorous of deceivers—his almost childlike belief in his royal destiny. Whether his great ancestor, Jalaluddin Muhammad Akbar, had inadvertently fostered this fatal hope, who was to say? She was, after all, a humble tamolan, a paan-woman whose only access to the goings-on at the Fort, was the discoursings between courtiers and customers who came to her canopied stall.

But a few days later she was summoned, by secret emissary of the Princess Begham Ain-e-Raushnaq to her gilded chambers at an hour well before dawn, an hour when princes slept and only palace servants were a-stir. The Princess was up and dressed in her quiet finery. A mild-mannered fawn-like being whose beauty called scant attention to itself until one looked again. And then one felt rather than saw, in the diffused light of her quiet diamonds, cool as starlight on an autumn night, the soft soul-light that infused her face. There was meekness in her gazelle eyes, a modest tilt to her small head, laden with the cascade of her heavy sidewise tiara and when she told her hand-maidens—'Go, I would be alone,' she made it sound like a submission rather than a command.

She beckoned her close, bade her sit, something no Princess ever did, and asked her her name.

'My name is Yamuni, my lady,' she'd answered, awed by the aura of this infinitely delicate woman.

'You are an artist of the betel leaf, Yamuni,' said the Princess. 'My lord is quite taken with your creations and we in the royal harem count you among our chosen purveyors of the paan.'

'It is your kindness, my lady,' she said, gladdened beyond words.

There was a silence. The Princess seemed to be caught in an inner disquiet. It took a few moments for her to speak.

'I have heard,' she said, 'that in ancient times, wives could wean away unfaithful husbands from other women by offering them paan...there is a mantra that pundits of your faith recommend...'

The Princess stopped speaking, as acute embarrassment seemed to overwhelm her. She half-lifted her gauzy head cloth to her flushed face in an unconscious gesture of shame, of humble confession, that won Yamuni's heart by its absolute womanliness in pain.

'There is such a mantra, my lady,' she replied. 'We call it the Vashikaran mantra. Our magi and ascetics say that if a crow be slain and its body buried in the ground and then dug up after a year and its bones then ground to powder and made into tiny pellets and those pellets hidden in a paan and fed to a man while reciting the Vashikaran mantra a hundred and eight times, the man will come forever into the encirclement of a woman's power.'

She pondered this a moment. Then said with such utter humility that Yamuni felt her heart go out to her.

'I ask you, as a woman, to do this for me. Please.'

There was the shine of tears in her glazed eyes and when she spoke it was in a small voice.

'Understand this—my lord is no philanderer, going after scores of women, as some do. But I love him much, more than I can tell, more than I can construe. It is no matter for a man to own many consorts, for women are like estates to be owned, the more the better. Why should this be at all amiss, I ask you? This is the way of nature, is it not?'

Yamuni did not think so but she knew her place. She might have said to her—'My lady Princess, consider the birds, each one stays loyal to its own mate. Consider the higher animals. It is man that uses his accursed brain to argue the strayings of his loins.' But she held her tongue.

'It is many days now since my master came to my bed,' the Princess said in a forlorn undertone that Yamuni had to strain her ears to catch. 'His three younger wives are more beauteous, far more than I can ever hope to be.'

She searched Yamuni's face for confirmation of this. Once again Yamuni did not agree. True, she reflected, my lord Khusrau's other wives, the Rajputani Jodha Bai, and those two others, the daughter of Vizeer Azim Khan and the daughter of Muqim, might have possessed straighter noses and finer-carved lips, thicker and longer hair and tinier waists but none of them had my lady's sweet aura, that soft vibration of mercy, that kindness of expression that is nobler far than mere fleshly symmetry. She said as much, in her own unpolished way.

But the Princess would not be consoled. 'You look on me with a woman's eye, Yamuni. May I call you Yamuni?'

May she? Yamuni trembled from head to foot at this graciousness of hers.

'You do not look on me as a man would. I have not that sap and scent of ripeness that men can smell.'

Yes, thought Yamuni. You smell of a temple's sacred incense when most men might prefer the armpit musk of female sweat! That is your tragedy. She still kept silent.

'I ask you to do this for me.' She seemed to require enormous mustering of will to put her thought in words. 'I ask you to arrange it all, the crow...' She flinched as she said this and forced herself to go on. 'I ask you to teach me the mantra and to create that paan for me.'

'My lady, the mantra I can't claim to know. It is probably in Sanskrit.'

'Alas, and I know only Persian,' she sighed.

In her mind Yamuni thought Sanskrit or Persian, we understand one another perfectly. The soul language of women exceeds the voice languages of men.

Nothing proved this better than her sad admission a moment later.

'It is not,' she said, 'that I begrudge them his love. It is not that I, churlish me, resent the joying he knows in their beds. A man needs his varieties of flavour, this I have been taught in the harem. Then what awful idolatry of mine is it, Yamuni, that I want him for my own exclusive self? Oh, I am a sinner to want this, but I cannot bear the agonizing pain of thinking he looks on another with favour. Oh, I sink and fail, I am reduced to nought, I have no worth in my eyes, I cannot eat or sleep. Is it love or is it my shame?'

'It is love, my lady. Radha too wanted her Krishna to be hers and hers alone.'

'Which of course he wasn't,' whispered the Princess. 'If I give you enough to go to Mathura or Vrindavan or even to distant Benaras and learn this mantra from some learned pundit, will you help me?'

'I will, my lady,' Yamuni promised. 'But will you be able to learn the Sanskrit mantra well yourself?'

'Then I shall serve him the paan and you shall recite the mantra,' the Princess smiled with such intimate fondness that Yamuni became her slave forever.

That evening she killed a crow, borrowing a bow and an arrow from a customer-suitor. But as it fell to the ground, reeling off its perch on the bough of the orchard's peepal tree, such a commotion arose in the branches and such an outcry of rage that Yamuni dropped her bow in surprise. The sky filled with batting wings, her ears resounded with the cawings of charging armies and till the next morning they sat on boughs and cornices and stone railings and minaret parapets, keeping vigil. By then there was absolute stillness, so sinister after that cawing agitation, that when Yamuni went to pick up the limp black body and bury it in a certain spot in the orchard, she felt the unnerving stare of scores of baleful eyes casting perdition upon her deed.

To Mathura she went, disguised. She learnt the power invocations, their accents and inflexions, their proper pauses and conjugations, their charged syllabic ascent. Then to Vrindavan she fled, when whisperings arose around her, questioning her identity. That centre of love and lore, where the plaints of longing women for men grown cool infused the very air and breathed around the scores of temples to the lover-god, that was where she hid herself.

It was a full long year by the time she returned to Agra. To learn, in the streets and squares, of what had befallen Prince Khusrau. Grown mistrustful of the plots being planted in the Prince's head by Man Singh, the Raja of Amber, his grandfather on his mother's side, and Aziz Khan Koka, the Prince's father-in-law and the lady Raushnaq's father, the Emperor, yes he—Nuruddin Mohammad Jahangir Padshah Ghazi—had commanded the Prince to stay confined to his palace suite along with his wives and never to go forth without hawk-like guards to watch and report on his every move. That the Prince had long lost his suave charm and grown peevish and jaundiced, prone to sink without warning into the deepest gloom, quite as his lady mother, the long-dead Man Bai or Shah Beghum, God rest her soul, she who'd killed herself when she could no longer abide the animosity between husband and son, had been.

'It is you, Yamuni, praise Allah!' murmured the Princess. 'Glad I am to see you, Yamuni. Now more than ever does my lord need saving. No, not from women, but the phantoms of his own melancholy fancies. He will not listen to me when I counsel caution and fortitude. When I plead with him to abandon his perilous projects, he flies into a rage. Does your mantra ensure a man's acceptance of sensible advice from a mere woman?'

'It is the Vashikaran mantra, my lady. It brings a man wholly under the influence of her who performs the ritual of the paan and the utterance of the syllables.'

Relief flooded the royal face. 'Then let us commence this ceremony as soon as you are ready, my Yamuni.'

'I am ready whenever you are, my lady.'

'Shall it be tonight?'

'Tonight if you wish it.'

But she had sensed a difficulty. The mantra has to be

recited 108 times while the paan was being offered. How was this agreement of timings to be worked out?

'I shall recite it 107 times while my lord is at his evening meal. The 108th time you shall offer him the paan while I utter the last repetition.'

The Princess regarded Yamuni with admiration. 'You are clever,' she commented.

'The poor are clever, my Princess. They have to be.'

'And the paan?' the Princess asked. 'You have the crowbone grains prepared?'

'That has been taken care of, my lady.'

'Is it not passing strange,' the Princess grew thoughtful, 'that we had to kill a bird to serve our cause of love? Perchance that bird had a love-mate too.' That was what her simple face, transparent as the dew-muslin indicated, though she did not voice the thought.

'Who knows these things, my lady?' Yamuni did not tell her the immense funereal outcry that had broken out in the branches that evening.

Khusrau was fretful, peeved by the music, by the meal, by the unexpected warmth of the Baisakh night, by the delay in the service. What a change had come over him! The furrowed brow, knit in perennial annoyance, the edge to his voice, the sting in his words, this was not the Prince Yamuni had known.

'Madam,' he jittered, irked. 'Will it be too much to entreat that you bestir your slothful self and hasten up this tiresome business of sweetmeats and paan? I long to retire.'

'As my lord desires.' The Princess stepped in. 'This paanwali is a tardy slob. Let me pluck this honour for my lowly self of offering you the paan myself.'

And as Yamuni, bowing low, holding the ornate silver tray, moved her lips the 108th time in the Vashikaran mantra, the Princess graciously culled a silver-foiled bida of paan, removed the ivory betel-pin, and with a worshipful expression of supplication, placed the paan in her husband's mouth.

He chewed on it with a disgruntled air. And as Yamuni was to recall later, perdition fall on her, what did she do? In her nervous tension as she watched her Princess's vigilant face, she unthinkingly went on repeating the syllables in her mind. On and on and on until about the 140th repetition, she realized in horror what she had done! By the time the Prince called for the spittoon she was shaking in trepidation, ready to flee the scene, desperate to get out of the Princess's sight, after the blunder she had committed. She had repeated that potent spell a hundred and forty times!

She only knew, as she sped away down the dark alleys outside the fort towards her house that she had to do penance. Plead with the gods who controlled the holy energies to forgive her careless lapse. For these esoteric incantations were not playthings to trifle with. She had to beg for the intercession of the divine lady Radha herself, guardian divinity of women in love.

If she had not taken herself to Mathura and Vrindavan in penitent pilgrimage she might have suffered the anguish of witnessing all that happened in the space of the next twelve days. In those twelve days Khusrau broke loose, reportedly during a visit to the tomb of his grandfather, Akbar, raised the standard of revolt against Jahangir, joined by malcontent Chughtai and Rajput chieftains, then rode hell-bent towards Lahore, hotly pursued by the armies of the recently appointed governor, Dilawar Khan. So much happened and so swiftly. Guru Arjan Dev of the Sikhs, whose blessings were bestowed on Khusrau en route to Lahore, incurring the permanent wrath of Jahangir, who had him slain. A heavy downpour of daylong rain, unusual in Baisakh, that mashed the battlefields north of the river Ravi into a clayey squelch.

Khusrau was brought back in chains. The appalled Agra multitudes watched as their favourite Prince staggered in at the head of his defeated army, manacled, shackled, in sodden, begrimed, ragged clothes, barefooted, unhelmeted, with matted locks, the very picture of a fakir who has looked into the well of death and is no longer of this world. And already the murmurs about his innocence, his saintliness, began arising, hushed whispers of lauding and lamenting, with the Empress's spies working overtime.

Yamuni, that paan-woman of simple faith, blamed it all on a mantra gone wrong. Her pilgrimage of penance clearly hadn't worked. For the latest reports in the streets and squares were of the manner in which Khusrau had to walk between rows of men, impaled upon gibbets on either side of the way, men screaming and howling in pain as the metal plunged through their anuses, their bowels, their stomachs, their lungs and all the way to their skulls and they slumped in death, a gory, bleeding mess of skewered flesh—all those loyal friends and chieftains who had marched behind his banner and cast their lot with his. Khusrau walked between the lines and having seen what he had to see, was made to abandon sight itself for good. For by his Emperor father's command, he was blinded. Thin wires drilled into his eyeballs in a manner of refined torture, designed to occasion the greatest pain. They said in the streets that the Prince uttered not a cry, showed not a flinch, not a wince, and they asked what more could be expected of a pir, a saint beloved of God. But how beloved? wept Yamuni night after night, as she sought her gods and plied them with entreaties, promises of sacrifices, fasts, renunciations. When the light of Khusrau's vision had almost departed the sanctum of his eyes, news spread like wild fire that the Emperor-father, he who had himself once rebelled against his own father in rash, younger times, had had a sudden change of heart and had sent his palace hakims to tend Khusrau's collapsed eyes. Then Yamuni knew her gods had heard. But no hakim or god could recall the light that had fled and it was bruited abroad that all that the Prince could faintly behold was the spectral presence of things.

Not that the world was much to look on, in the dungeon in which he was cast. Guarded and forbidden all company. Denied all ordinary comforts and abandoned by all his wives at the behest of the Emperor. Save one who refused to leave. And Yamuni felt a sinking in her heart each time she thought of the botched and bungled mantra that she and that one had conspired to work.

It was many months later that a man, posing as a paan trader, brought her a message. And obeying the summons in the dead of night, throwing all caution to the winds and all regard of personal safety, she made her way through the secret entrance to the dungeons, the mouth of the tunnel in the bel forest guarded by sentries night and day.

She came away disappointed but knew what she had to do if she was to gain access into the tunnel leading to the dungeons. The same two sentries guarded the entrance in the bel forest every night. Orgies were not her talent but paan might numb their brains and perchance their loins as well. Paan stuffed with opium in the pouch formed between the left and the right lobes of the leaf cone. How had he looked when she had explained the niceties of betel-confecting to her Prince? His face came back to her with such a sharp pang of pain that she was stunned by the paralyzing knowledge that the Vashikaran mantra was working in more ways than one. This thralldom was for life, for good or ill. All means were fair so long as she could only come into his presence. Even working her charms on Javed Khan and Mansoor Alam who guarded the entrance to the tunnel, letting them toy with her body, shove their roving hands where they pleased and in succession probe her interiors with the tumid tools of this trading and do their business and pronounce her cheap at the price she quoted. So long as she could, in the act of lulling their suspicions, give them the kiss of sleep, a mouth to mouth love game of paan coquetry that slipped the dose of opium into their slobbering mouths.

It was when they had sunk into sodden stupor that she entered the tunnel and groped her way forward down its damp passageway to the staircase leading up to the dungeons. It was a route she would memorize and take many times in the weeks to come and she would pause in the darkness to rearrange her tousled hair, her tumbled-about garments, fresh with the reek of recent copulation. She would produce a tiny bottle of jasmine itr and dab it on the inside of her wrists, the slope of her temples and the folds of her headcloth and the drapes of her skirt and even the carved loops of the bangles she wore and the anklets on her feet.

'Yamuni! I knew it. I knew you would come. I knew you would find a way.'

The Princess's welcome was heart-warming. 'We bid you welcome to our royal palace.'

Yamuni looked around and checked the Princess's face for marks of bitterness as she uttered these words but found instead only her usual sad, gentle friendliness.

It was a better class of dungeon, very sparsely furnished, not the bare, dingy cavern-like darkness she had come expecting. On one of the two pallet beds on the floor a man lay, turned away to the wall. There was a low divan with a rough rug spread on it. Light came in from a pair of long, narrow slits high up in the stone wall. There were iron rings to hold flaming torches and oil lamps in a niche. There were a few pitchers and carafes. A prayer mat, prayer beads, a few books.

'Wherever you are, my lady, that place becomes a palace for me,' Yamuni whispered, overcome by emotion.

The Princess's hair was streaked with grey and it lent its own starlight to her pale, drawn face as her diamonds once had. She might have been a homely seamstress or a female hammam help from her clothes but for the nobility of her face which nothing could take away. As for the Prince, who turned over in his sleep and faced the two women, oblivious of them, Yamuni did not dare look on him at first. When she coerced her eyes to do so she saw a greyed man, thin as a draggled crow, a permanent frown carved on his fretful brow. Her heart turned over. Her breath stopped. This lined, caved-in form in its rough, grimy tunic could ignite such a stab of longing in her, it was like the twist of a sharp dagger in her gut.

'No doubt you heard of it all,' said the Princess. 'He calls me Raushni Mahal now. The Light of the Palace—you can see this Palace for what it is worth. He calls me that ever since he was blinded by his father's orders.'

'You have stayed here all this while?' asked Yamuni in a tremulous whisper.

'Yes,' said the Princess. 'Except when the Emperor decides to sally forth on a formal occasion. Then he needs to make a public spectacle of my lord as an example to all traitors—so my lord has to walk shackled at the rear of the procession. The guards bring him back and he collapses onto his bed and lies in a faint for the rest of the day.'

'I have heard of it, my lady,' said Yamuni. 'But do you know what the common people say when they see my lord Khusrau shuffling along like a common felon in shackles behind the Emperor's cavalcade? They say—there goes our saint Prince, our pure one.'

Even in the light of the dim oil lamp Yamuni could see the gladdened flush on the Princess's face.

'May God bless you, my friend,' she whispered. 'It will bring much joy to his broken heart when I tell him this. But I have troubled you to undertake this visit to our chamber of grief, Yamuni, to ask another favour of you.'

'It is for you to command me, my lady,' murmured Yamuni. 'This slave is here to serve you—if it lies within my power.'

The Princess cast an anxious glance at her sleeping husband and said, 'Hush, I cannot take the risk of speaking here. Come to the ghusal chamber—we can talk there.'

Yamuni followed her to a tiny hollow space adjoining the

dungeon chamber which had been got up as a bathing space with large pitchers and basins, platters of soap-stone and a privy. A black as pitch place, foul smelling and unventilated.

'I apologize for the filth of this place, Yamuni,' said the Princess in a small voice. 'It is the only place private enough.'

'You shame me, Princess, by apologizing,' said Yamuni.

'Then listen, we don't have much time. He may waken any moment. The ways of this court are strange. First the Emperor had him blinded, then he was remorseful—we can only interpret it as remorse, however perverse—and he sent his physicians to try and save my lord's sight, which they failed to do except just a whit. First he had him thrown into this dungeon, asked his wives to abandon him, tormented him in every which way. Then suddenly she—Nur Jahan—sends for him and asks him to marry her daughter from her earlier marriage, that Laadli Bano who hasn't been able to find a groom. And she promises to rescue him from this hell, even to ensure that he ascends the throne after his father departs this world. But he is stubborn as flint, my madman husband. He is bitter, ah, so bitter after my sister-wives, those other three obeyed the Emperor and left him. He clings to me as a shadow clings to the pillar that casts it. He answered her with all the concentrated bitterness of his torment. He said, "Lady Mother, there is but one woman in this whole world whom I honour enough to call my wife and that is the one who has been by my side through these dark days when God himself, may the blasphemy be forgiven, seemed to have forgotten me. The daughter of Aziz Khan Koka, my senior-most, my only wife now and forever. No throne can tempt me and as for relief from my condition, I am content to remain in it if I do so in her company." That said, he sent the messenger away. Now do you even begin to understand the peril to which he has exposed himself? She—Nur Jahan—is vengeful. Who can dream of slighting her? And slighted she is. Enraged. No good will come of this refusal, as I wept and told my lord. Only more misfortune, only greater pain than body or soul can endure. I begged him on my knees to accede to the Empress's wishes but he is adamant. Will you, my Yamuni, find another mantra to persuade him?'

Yamuni was torn between astonishment and amusement.

'There is no mantra needed to induce a man to add to the sum of the women in his bed, my lady, begging your pardon,' she said. 'And strange are the ways of court indeed. Last time you asked me to find a mantra to keep your lord your exclusive one. This time you ask me to persuade him to accept another woman.'

'Do not quibble with me, my friend,' the Princess said sadly. 'I want only my lord's safety. And I have grown in love, here in the confines of this hell, watching his suffering and nursing him. There have been times when the Emperor has gone on one of his long hunts and had my lord walled in, and I have chosen to be walled in with him. I know now that the noblest love is to desire the satisfaction of the one to whom we have given our best. And I want my lord to recover the flavour of another woman in his bed...so that... so that...he can get used to the idea and...and...'

'What is this you are asking me to do, my lady?' Yamuni was aghast, stupefied.

'It is exactly what you understand, my Yamuni. Exactly that. Whom could I ask but you? I have it all planned. I shall vanish into this ghusal-khana and you shall...'

Yamuni was bewildered.

'I cannot, my lady,' she flushed.

'Why not?'

'I am not worthy, my lady. A paan-woman. No royalty.'

'You are my closest friend, the sharer of my secrets, what matters it if you were not born in a palace? There be some here who are not fit to be honest paan-women but some accident of birth has put them in a palace.'

'But my lord may not...may not...'

'That is for you to manage.'

What is she expecting of me? That I turn seductress of her husband? Yamuni looked helplessly at the Princess.

'Why are you doing this, my lady?' she asked.

'Haven't you understood a word of what I have been saying all this time? My lord Khusrau's life is in danger if he goes on refusing to marry Laadli Bano. The Empress won't spare him. And Khurram, his half-brother, will surely have him slain unless he can secure Nur Jahan's protection and patronage. I know it like the lines on my palm. He's got to marry Laadli. That is our only hope. But he swears he will not look at another woman. He swears he can't. I want him to realize that he can. I beg you, Yamuni, on my bended knees, as I begged him to take heed of this marriage proposal. It isn't a choice between women—it is a choice between life and death. Remember, if it comes to pass that my lord is killed, reflect how you shall feel...to think you might have helped to prevent it. Yamuni, friend of my heart, what more can I do to persuade you? I have not gold on me or jewels to give you...'

'For shame, my lady!' exclaimed Yamuni. 'That you should imagine I value such inducements when your word alone shall suffice. But how…in what way…?'

A faint sound in the adjoining dungeon made them rush out of the ghusal-khana. Khusrau was awake, sitting upright in his pallet bed. He gazed in her direction with empty sightless eyes. He held his head slightly tilted, as though listening for presences rather than seeing them.

'Who is that with you, beghum?'

'It is Yamuni, my old friend, my lord. Do you remember the beauteous paan-woman Yamuni, she that created those enchanting confections of the betel leaf? We used to call her the enchantress of the leaf in the harem. Believe me, she is as beauteous as she was then and an enchantress still.'

Khusrau looked peevish. 'What blabber is this, beghum?' he grumbled. 'I am thirsty. I must have water.'

The Princess poured out a gobletful of water from an earthen carafe and put it in Yamuni's benumbed hand, prodded her forward.

'As you wish, my lord,' she said calmly.

Yamuni stepped up, her feet unsteady, to the near-blind Prince. She held the goblet out to Khusrau.

He sniffed. Looked at her with mistrust. 'Are these the hands that made paan for us once?'

'Yes, my lord. It is I, Yamuni. Can you see me, sire?'

'I have no wish to see you, girl. Too much have these eyes seen—they do not desire to see anything more of this despicable world. But can you see me, girl? What do your eyes make of this destroyed heap of a man, once a Prince?'

'I cannot see you, my lord,' whispered Yamuni truthfully,

'for my eyes are misted with tears.'

He drank off the water in a gulp, handed the goblet back.

'Then I have an advantage over you, girl,' he pronounced wryly. 'For even with these ruined eyeballs I can see you.'

'How so, my lord?'

'I see you, yes. I see you by the rustle of your garment, by the way the vibration of your tread travels across the ground. Do you have flowers on you, girl?'

'No, my lord. It is only itr.'

'Jasmines,' he murmured. 'My favourite flower. It is ages since I stepped into a real garden. Come here. Let me get a whiff of you. Let me breathe you. Where is this itr? On your wrists, your ear-lobes?'

She extended both her hands to him, held them, palms turned upwards, to his face. She bent low to allow his nostrils close to her ears, first the one and then the other.

'What sound is that?' he asked, his expression suddenly vigilant. 'Are those horses' hoofs? Far away, miles maybe?'

'No, my lord,' she whispered. 'That is my pulse beating.'

His breath in her hair was too disturbing, filling her with the pain of impossible desire.

He let her hands go. 'Go, girl,' he said gruffly.

She was glad to get away. All this while the Princess had stood silent, satisfied. She came quickly forward to lead Yamuni back into the tunnel that opened into the bel forest.

'It will take a little time,' was all she said.

But the Princess was wrong. It never went beyond the fragrance of jasmine or rose or mogra or monsoon-wet earth— all the fragrances that Yamuni bought up from an itr dealer in the Meena Bazaar. Khusrau possibly did not think her anything beyond a travelling garden of inaccessible flowers. The Princess was getting anxious.

'We haven't much time,' she jittered. 'The messengers have come again with the marriage proposal and my lord has been offensive to a really extreme extent. There is but one thing we must do. You must impersonate me, Yamuni. You must wear my clothes, musky with my body presences, and then you must creep into his bed when he is half asleep. Only when it is over shall I enter the chamber and prove to him that another woman in his bed is no different from the one he stubbornly refuses to leave. But he must be half asleep.'

'An opium paan might be useful, my lady,' murmured Yamuni nervously, ruefully reflecting on the uses to which the opium paan had been already put.

So on the very next night, bereft of all scents, cleansed of the odours of the guards at the mouth of the tunnel in the bel forest, Yamuni donned the clothes of the Princess, who retired into the ghusal-khana. Khusrau lay with his face to the wall as was his habit. After his partial blinding, he often forgot to close his eyes in sleep and it made for a sinister picture. Yamuni was glad he had his face turned away as she lowered herself into the pallet-bed, timidly stretched herself out and placed a tentative arm on his shoulder. He responded involuntarily, turned to face her, drew her close. She felt she would melt in the intimacy of the embrace and waited to taste his mouth with a fervour that frightened her. Her breath came short and fast as her tongue moved into the cave of his mouth and at that very instant Khusrau pushed her away with a force too violent for her to withstand, a push that hurled her away onto the ground as he shot up bolt upright in bed, shouting curses:

'Slut! Lane-cat! Begone!'

She was weeping, both from unrequited desire as from the shame of this thwarted enterprise. She covered her face with her headcloth and sobbed into its folds, 'I only want to lie beside you, master, even if it be in a grave! I wanted nothing else save to serve my lady and you...'

The sound of her sobbing brought in the Princess who came rushing in from the adjoining ghusal-khana.

'You, madam!' stormed Khusrau. 'This be your scheme, I know it! What think you of me, that Khusrau, being blinded and led about in chains, is a captive of this body that he has come to dread? Think you that all the fleshly sufferings he has known have not disenchanted him of this body forever! Know this, madam, Khusrau is master of his will and his flesh, even if that flesh be torn to shreds!'

The Princess made an effort to calm him down. 'Hush,' she begged. 'You are so wrong, my lord. Yamuni forgot herself for love of you. You little know the effect you have on us women!'

'Quiet, woman!' thundered Khusrau. 'I may not have eyes but I can see through your wiles. Understand this, beghum, no power on earth, neither you nor your Empress can make Khusrau take another woman. As for you, wanton hussy, take yourself away! I spit on you!'

The din had brought in the guards on the inner side of the dungeon. As Yamuni was led away by them, she left the Princess, cowering on the stone flags of the chamber floor, shaking in panic.

And though the ravishment that followed, at the hands of many men who made show of guarding the prisons, left her torn and battered, word of her plight had travelled to Nur Jahan, who sent instructions to have her conducted to her royal chambers where she was made to confess her visits to Khusrau's dungeon, her account endorsed by the outer guards who exposed her as a willing wanton, a practising whore who was in the habit of sleeping with them and perchance with lord Khusrau too, may Allah forgive them for failing to fulfil their duties.

'It is well,' pronounced the Empress, well pleased. 'Let the court and the common people be advised that their precious prince, the one they call a saint, is not above whoring with a common tart. Let everyone know this and we shall see to it that this fact is writ in the pages that bear witness to the happenings of our reign, be it in ink or in stone.'

Yamuni was released after she had, on pain of death, confessed that what the Empress said was true, after she had been paraded before the royal durbar as the harlot who visited Prince Khusrau in his dungeon and who had been his moll.

What to say of those times! Her people disowned her, her father and brothers, her very mother cast her out. Agra trod her underfoot, scoffed and slandered whichever way she turned. A sacred hospice to a pir took her in, pitying her condition, for she was afflicted with many inner wounds. The holy hakims there treated her with herbs and medicaments and amulets and charms and blown-on holy water and their prayers. Then they put her on a cart bound for the east.

She did not know know where she was going. She had no skill save paan-making and the paan-woman's repartee and that other skill with men that life had taught her and which she was now loath to use, so repelled was she by men. But there was one other thing she had learnt in childhood, from her visits to her village—how to make a bareja. A bareja was a frame-house made of straw, a sort of green tent in which the paan vine grew. People of the Tamoli caste knew how to make it, only Yamuni was now an outcast. But who in Unnao or Lucknow or Rae Bareli or Kanhapur knew her? The paan vine needed hot, steamy summers of the east and she became a nomadic bareja-making hand, going where work and the season took her. Eastwards she went as the years passed and the marks of time travelled across her worn face and her work-roughened hands. How many seasons or years went by she had no record of until one afternoon, working in the fields along the broad, shaded highway that swept across the vast plains of the land, their paths crossed again, the Princess's and hers. This time in the form of a mighty, procession of carts and horses and palanquins and slow-treading elephants with curtained howdas on their swaying backs.

What is this?—was what each village asked. Was this a new feast or strange campaign? Those in the know told the milling crowds of men and women who had abandoned their work in the fields, their ploughing and sowing, their forges and workshops, and rushed to see, that this was the body of that tragic prince, Khusrau, bound for distant Ilahabad. That holy one, Khusrau, the saintly, the one of unshakeable principle, the innocent one sacrificed at the altar of history, as the innocent are.

Yamuni could not believe her ears. She could hardly catch what the horsemen were saying as they pushed the crowds back with their lances, so loud was the drumming of her heart. The catafalque, elevated on its bullock cart, came to rest beneath an old peepal tree and the horsemen had a hard time of it for the crowds grew in number, plunged forwards in their scores and hundreds, trying to strew rose petals on the ground where the bier stood, rushing up with their joss sticks and their pots of Ganga water, Hindus and Muslims, weavers and coppersmiths and ironmongers and peasants. The noise was so great and the lamentation, you might have thought it was Muhorrum day and a mourning procession, in a trance of anguish, weeping over a lost battle and its slaughtered heroes.

There was just this thought in her pounding heart. Somewhere in this cavalcade of death, in one of these dozen curtained palanquins, was her lady Princess and she had to find her. She had a night to do it in but there were guards all around. And no longer did she possess that ready facility with guards that she once had and this was no secret place.

However, nature came to her help and late that night, she saw a group of veiled women emerge from the palanquins and head for the dark fields—for even royal women must do what ordinary mortals and beasts, all those trapped in this bodily prison must. And when the group reassembled to return to the palkis she mingled with them, the Princess's handmaidens and begged to have a word with her. They would not heed Yamuni and Yamuni pleaded so hard she might have raised her voice, for suddenly a lady, veiled and cloaked from head to foot, stopped, turned and cried, 'Who's that?'

'It is I, Yamuni!' she was weeping in her desperation and the Princess, recognizing her voice, hissed, 'Silence! Come near. Let her, my ladies. I beg you.'

And they, possibly in pity at their lady's bereaved condition, grew quiescent, put Yamuni in the middle of their cluster and thus did Yamuni walk with them, likewise veiled, alongside the Princess and thus did she manage to ascend the elephant's back that held the curtained howdah in which the Princess was travelling.

'Leave us alone,' pronounced the Princess and the handmaiden who was to share the space with her lady Princess quietly moved into another palanquin and none of the guards were any the wiser.

And thus did Yamuni learn all that had transpired.

'Ah, Yamuni, my own, my friend,' lamented the Princess. 'Five years and what years! Long did Asaf Khan strive to prevail on my lord Khusrau to give his consent to the Empress's marriage proposal but you know my lord as well as I do. What was destined to happen did happen. The Empress married her daughter Laadli off to Prince Shahryar instead and retribution visited us in another form. For Khurram, ever wary of my lord's standing with the people, ever jealous, devised his plans. What is my lord's failing? That he has been too brave, too noble, too good to make the small durbar a comfortable place for jealous rivals, for surely such is the fate of the truly excellent.'

'It is indeed, my lady,' murmured Yamuni.

'Then Khurram asked the Emperor, his father, for custody of my lord. The indignity of it! As though my lord was a slave, an object to be transferred from owner to owner, but such it was. The Emperor agreed and we had to journey all the way to Burhanpur in the Deccan where Khurram had my lord imprisoned in quarters of his own and me in a chamber nearby. Though, Allah be thanked, our chambers communicated by a passage and we had the consolation of a few paltry hours together, the greatest mercy of our last days.'

'A great mercy, true, my lady.'

'It would have come to pass sooner or later. I found my lord strangled in his bed one morning. His body had been laid out straight on the bed and Khurram's messengers conveyed the news that my lord had died of the qalanj, having suffered acute pains of the stomach. But the truth got out—how Raza Bahadur, himself one of Khurram's accursed slaves, broke down the door to my lord's chamber, forced an entry along with his minions and slew him most brutally. Even so, one of the foul wretches who helped in the deed, let out the fact that my lord, near-blind though he was, fought like a tiger, alone against many, and was overpowered and throttled! Ah, my soul shudders, Yamuni! I fall into a dead faint many times in a day to think of it! The hakims say—do not think, for that way madness lies but how can I not relive his last, his horrid, fearsome plight in all its detail every moment of the day?'

The Princess wept on Yamuni's shoulder.

'Now we are bound for Ilahabad at Nur Jahan's behest. My lord's body was taken out of its grave and is being dispatched to Ilahabad to be buried beside the grave of his mother Shah Beghum in a bagh there, for the powers that be dare not allow his grave to exist in Agra or anywhere near Agra. For from distant outposts of the Mughal realms have protests come, yes, even from faraway Gujarat, that this was murder of a good man, an innocent one, a man of honour. They'd started lighting lamps on his makeshift grave, covering it with sacred sheets and with garlands and crowds from villages had started coming on pilgrimage and praying at it. They would have made a pir of him had they had their way, these peasants and alley-folk. It might have become too hard to handle so here we are—being sent to Ilahabad for burial, my lord first, me next.'

'Oh do not say that, my Princess,' exclaimed Yamuni.

'Why ever not? It is said that empty graves have been kept ready at that bagh in Ilahabad. Who is to lie in them except those who were dear to my lord—his sister, me, our children? I now await my end, Yamuni.'

Yamuni's mind was made up. She had not known how dearly she loved this bereaved woman, this princess of grief.

'When do you expect to meet your end, lady?' she asked calmly.

'Any time after he is buried.'

'Then, my lady, that time shall never come,' intoned Yamuni with a decisiveness of voice that came as a surprise to the Princess.

'We have exchanged clothes before,' said Yamuni. 'You have become the poor paan-woman and I have become a princess.'

'It failed,' said the princess.

'It failed with him. It won't this time. You can get away, my lady. Get away and travel by country routes and across the fields eastwards and wait for me.'

The Princess was taken aback. 'What are you saying? That you shall impersonate me in this cavalcade? You are bound to be caught. This time it will be a worse plight than then.'

'I care not,' said Yamuni. 'It was bad enough then. It can be no worse. If death should come, my lady, so be it. My family disowns me. I have no life to treasure. I travel from farm to farm, building frame shelters for the paan vine. There is no future to tempt me. Far be it to die in the sweet knowledge that my death has been useful, if not my life. But, if my sense is right, nothing of that kind shall befall me. I know the secrets of poisoning the paans I make and where to find the poisonous herbs. I carry them on my person— what else is there for a lone woman to do? Perchance I am caught, I know how to release myself from life, long before the Emperor's henchmen do.'

It took her long to convince the Princess but she succeeded. And the Princess's handmaidens, if they understood, by common consensus it seemed, said nothing. For in their hearts they too believed Khusrau to be a blameless martyr. They too believed that to serve the soul of a holy one was to accumulate merit in the eyes of God. As indeed did the common people for everywhere the cavalcade stopped the crowds continued to swarm, little shrines came up, makeshift structures of veneration to a man soon becoming a legend.

As for herself, in the garments of royalty, in the veiled drapes of mourning, she retreated into the essential recesses of another's identity, weeping for another's loss and conforming to the requirements of another's station. There was little to choose between the fate of a homeless, ravished paan-woman and a bereaved and death-haunted princess. She bided her time as the slow procession wended its way down the broad highway towards Ilahabad, well satisfied that each day allowed her princess to put a greater distance between herself and death. The moment of discovery would come, this she knew.

It came on the day Khusrau's remains were to be interred in the fresh grave prepared for it. The bagh lay in a lonely expanse, far from the riverine city that encircled the fort. She had prayed to her several gods and was going through the motions of the princess's prayers when a commotion outside disturbed her and before she could draw her veil across her face, a burly form strode into her private tent. Seeing her in prayer, he waited. So did she. She felt his eyes drill into her shoulder blades as she held herself in the position of prayer, praying to the god who exceeds all others, her own as well as the princess's, to keep up her spirits in this moment of discovery. She did not know the exactitude and niceties of the princess's prayer, its pauses and submissions, its conventions of movement and stillness. And it was this that made the intruder watch her with greater attention. It was this that made him spring on her before the act of prayer concluded.

'You are not she!' was what he hissed.

'Else, would you have laid hands on her thus?' asked Yamuni impudently. 'No, I am not she.'

He bared his teeth in a snarl. He drew his sword. 'Who are you, woman?'

'A woman. But not the one you came looking for. But you may have the favour of drawing your brave warrior's sword on this mere woman, for such I know is your intent.'

'Who are you? Why are you here?'

'I am a tamolan, your honour. A paan-woman, friend of my Princess and well-loved of her.'

'Where is the Princess?'

'The one you came to slay, by your secret royal orders? She is far away where you or your Emperor shall never find her. Slay me in her stead and tell your Emperor that my lord Khusrau was a saint for whom peasants and paan-women could lay down their lives.'

He looked on her uncertainly, then slowly lowered his

sword.

'You are the brazen hussy who used to visit the dungeons of Agra fort? The slut Khusrau slept with?'

'That is what you think. It is what has been bruited abroad. Believe it if you despise him. Do not believe it if you have any regard for him.'

It was a question rather than an instruction. And it had its effect. The man stood still in uncertainty, then came forwards and whispered, 'I do not believe it, madam.'

'Then why do you come here with drawn sword?'

'It is my job, madam.'

She swirled her chadar imperiously about her form. 'Then get on with it and do your job, my brave man,' she sneered.

He moved a step closer till he was bending over her and muttered, 'My lord Khusrau was my hero but this is my assignment. Fear not, madam.'

Then he raised his voice and roared, 'An imposter! A fraud!—as Allah is my witness!'

He held her arm in an iron grip and dragged her towards the curtained opening of the tent. She lost her footing and fell and he did not stop but dragged her forward, her cloak falling away, her hair coming loose. He shouted, 'Guards! See who I have here! A she-devil in human form!'

'This,' he roared, 'is the infamous tamolan of Agra, Khusrau's moll! Pretending to be Khusrau's wife! Now, shall we slay the slut or shall we hold her hostage till the lady we wish to find comes forward? Speak, where is she?'

Yamuni rose to her feet, dusted herself superciliously and remained silent. A crowd had converged on her, guards in Mughal arms, hawkers, masons, flower-women from around the mosque, her shrill handmaidens.

'How did you let this happen?' The Mughal soldier turned on one of the hand-maidens and thundered.

She trembled, sank to her knees, and spoke in fright, 'I know nothing, master guard. I swear on the Book, I know nothing.'

'You lie, whore!' he shouted. 'And you shall all share her fate, you that let Khusrau's wife get away. You shall all be put to the sword!'

A collective cry arose from the women milling around.

'But wait,' he spat. 'We must report this to Agra before we take action. Let a courier be sent for, a horseman of speed...'

'Take them away!' shouted the thwarted assassin. 'Throw them in the tomb chamber of Khusrau's mother. But not that one, the accursed paan-woman. She shall be bound and gagged and kept under observation in my own tent'.

It was after night had fallen and the fires that had been lit in small makeshift hearths all around the camp had died down and the women locked in Shah Beghum's tomb chamber been given food and water, that the man who had come to slay her approached her cautiously. Sternly he unbound and ungagged her, motioning absolute silence. In silence he led her through a clump of dense trees in the bagh to where a hillock of crumbled masonry, overgrown with weeds and littered with camp-refuse, stood.

'Go,' he said, 'go now. This tunnel leads to the fort. It has only recently been completed. Make haste and god speed you. I have sent spies ahead and made arrangements. She is waiting for you in a boat bound for Benaras. Go.'

She stopped only to bless him with her eyes before she

vanished into the mouth of the tunnel. The darkness did not scare her, used as she was to groping her way forwards, feeling along the wall and placing one foot after the other. The thing was to keep going forward, step following step, even if it took hours, even if the drumming of one's own heartbeat frightened one.

Day was breaking by the time light hove in sight, a dazzle of smoky dawn-grey that stunned the sight and almost blinded her for a few moments before the world resolved itself.

On the ghats of Benaras, in the noisy confusion of chanting and the blowing of conchs and the ringing of temple bells and the cries of garland makers and pyre-wood hawkers and hubbub of pilgrims, they had their heads shaved by a ritual barber. They had already discarded their former clothes and selves and stood draped in rough unstitched cotton, the saree pulled close over their heads. Begging for alms did not prove as difficult for them, for no words were needed, just the extension of a palm sufficed and more was the miracle that the gesture was heeded and coins dropped into supplicating palms, proving to their sore hearts that sometimes, though not often, speechless appeals were heard. The seasons drifted away like cast-away flowers borne on the river's stream. The days and nights dissolved and the years. Pilgrims brought news that made them weep—of the wholesale slaughter of all Khusrau's children—the quiet Dawar Baksh, the noisome Buland Akhtar, the young Hushang Mirza, even the little Shahzadi Hoshmand Bano Beghum. They learnt of the construction of a mighty monument above Khusrau's tomb. And some distance away, in sneering imperial proclamation of Khusrau's low association with a shabby paan-woman, another tomb popularly called the Tamolan's tomb. In the grounds of the well laid-out bagh waited a few more empty tombs—which suggested that the hunt for them was still on and the destination chalked out in advance. But the Princess spoke of returning incognito to her father Aziz Khan Koka's family when she felt the end approaching, that she could lie in a grave and become one with the silent earth. And Yamuni knew she would die, like a good Hindu, in Benaras and her ashes would go downstream on the Ganga's swelling waves and become one with the river's perennial waters.

And so be lost to history, each in her way.

SIX

The Drawbridge

*T*he very first morning he took a little walk round the Civil Lines market and bought a diary and an ADD gel pen and a couple of refills. Aside from letters home, he hadn't written so much as a page and now the weight of the diary and pens felt heavier than the heaviest artillery he'd ever handled in the old days.

The reason why he opted to arrive two days earlier, on the 12th of August rather than the morning of the 14th and the reason why he'd chosen to check into a hotel in the Civil Lines than in one of the Fort's guest apartments, was that he needed a no-man's-land. A neutral space in which to abdicate his defences and come to terms with what he planned to tell them. His Post-Traumatic Stress Disorder had lasted forty years—probably the term didn't exist in 1962—and he had come to a vital decision.

It had been hard to explain all this to his host and only the secrecy of his arrival and the anonymity of his assumed name in the hotel's guest register made sure of forty-eight hours of desperately-arranged solitude in which he could delve into the dark recesses of his denials and put it all in words. Later, he'd phone the Colonel, maybe on the 14th evening and inform him of his arrival ahead of schedule. He didn't quite know what reason he'd give but he was sure that having uttered in words what he had set himself to utter, he'd be capable of any kind of honesty on earth.

He'd had some sort of premonition, when he'd accepted Colonel Baghel's invitation to visit the Allahabad Fort and address the men on Independence Day that the untold story he'd carried these many years would have to be told. Something his mind had locked away had to be exhumed and admitted, not to family, not to personal friends—that was out of the question—but to fellow soldiers and so maybe to the future. It had troubled him. It had involved him in inner arguments that refused to go away, pushed him to the edge, compelled him to confront difficult things of conscience and some questions he'd kept for later—how were human beings capable of such extreme courage and how were the same guys capable of the most grisly depravities? And more centrally, what complicated motivations activated when wars were fought for ideas—if they ever were fought for ideas alone! And some essential things about being human. He'd lately begun reading history and especially war-histories. Thucydides, Sun Tzu, the lot. And he, never remarkable as a thinking or reading sort of man.

He entered his room, laid it all on the writing desk and sat looking at it for ten minutes. He had dug up his old papers and now he leafed through them, their blue-black ink faded on paper turned yellow with age. Major Chaudhary was killed on the 21st, he'd reported to the General. Majors Bashyan, Lts Naveen Kohli and Gurdas and approximately 200 men are still missing. I am hopeful that most of them will turn up. The names of those shot by the Chinese at Hathung La I don't know but two of my boys, Balbir Singh and Narain Singh I distinctly saw. Dilbagh with his boys from Lumpu has also managed to come out through Bhutan. Sub Major with boys at Tawang arrived back safely. The Brigade Head-quarters except for the Brigadier has come out mostly through Bhutan. In the other battalions 2 Rajputs are the worst affected as so far only one officer and about forty men have come out. 1/9 Grenadiers have suffered about 50 per cent casualties. Majors Charack, Siri Kant, Pawar, Minwala, Lts Didi and Kutaya have come out. In 4 Grenadiers, except for Lt Rao, who was at Khinzemane, all other officers have come out with 65 to 70 per cent of the men. Among the wounded or taken prisoner are Brigadier Dalvi, Lt Col. Rattan Singh, Lt Col Balwant Singh Ahluwalia, Lt Col M.S. Rikh—all our commanders of the three battalions on the Namka Chu river.

Also killed, on the 20th on the Namka Chu front was the General's own nephew, Captain Mahabir Prasad, that gallant, shining boy, but this he had not known at the time of reporting. He had accordingly expressed the hope that Mahabir too had managed to come out. There were many more who did not manage to come out. Out of twelve hundred, four hundred men lay dead and a hundred and ninety officers, the rest taken captive.

But this other was a story he'd told so often it had become his truth. Even his reference point of self after '62. A thrilling story of marches and counter-marches. Of villages that gave them refuge. The uniform he had changed into was that of a tall Chinese soldier—must have been a Han. The villagers had shot him dead with his own gun. He'd sent signals through bird calls he had learnt. That's how the twelve of them came together—all wearing Chinese uniforms that the village provided, in addition to the makki they ate. Of the woman who washed and dressed his suppurating feet.

Now more than ever it mattered that he should win this war. But his mind always came to a grinding halt, no matter how hard he worked at it. Every one of the others was dead. The story could die quietly with him. For some reason it had to come out, this unquiet truth that was deeper than all his several truths.

But dealing with a resistant artificial memory made his throat go tight with animal panic. The perilous terrain opened before him, potent with menace, and rather than hurtle headlong down that cliff into the blinding depths, his first impulse was to defer the threat by grabbing the complimentary volume on the Allahabad Fort that Col Baghel had couriered him along with his invitation a month ago.

An arty sort of book. All breathtakingly beautiful paintings, Mughal, Company School, and period photographs on glossy paper. He turned the pages, glad of escape. Read the names of the painters who made the Allahabad Fort a palette of mood and personality. Sita Ram, James Arden Crommelin, Robert Smith, Thomas Danielle. Cool pastel evening-scapes engaging stone and water. Clouds dramatic in monsoon skies, old country-boats caught bobbing on tangled streams or moored against a background of towering battlements. Opulent interiors and tapestried gate-houses—was the Fort really like that in some remote time? The red stone of the Rani Mahal, languid site of music and dance, still breathing a sense of captive perfumes leached into the stone. The tiers on tiers of the Chalees Sutoon. He turned the pages, read the text alongside the colour plates. Read closely if only to put off the assignment he had set himself. Stories about the Fort. Some of them cute and folklorey. About the sage whose name was Mukund Brahmachari and who, the legend claimed, had been Emperor Akbar in a previous incarnation. A Hindu holy man who'd swallowed a cow's hair by mistake as he quaffed his milk and who'd then realized that suicide was the only way out of the defiled condition to which he had fallen. He jumped from the ancient Akshaya-vat, the indestructible banyan tree, into the waters of the river—though a parallel tradition held that he had immolated himself—wishing in his last moments to be born a Mussalman Emperor of India, seeing that after swallowing any part of the sacred body of a cow, he knew himself forever excluded from Hinduhood in all subsequent incarnations. To be reborn as Akbar, that paragon of liberal monarchs, who recognized the site of his previous existence when he visited it and decided to build his fort there!

He read on, amused. Alongside a full page colour plate of Prayag-raja, the city-god, another folksy myth. How the poverty stricken Raja of Jhunsi, on the far bank of the river, had nothing of value to bring to the Mughal Emperor when Akbar held his grand durbar and gave audience to the local kings and chieftains of the area. And how, his own minister Birbal—the same Birbal who later joined Akbar's court and became the Emperor's jesting companion—suggested he bring a large silver platter bearing worship things, tulsi leaves, Ganga water, a tiny silver trowel, for the Emperor instead. And how

Birbal advised him to answer the Emperor's curious question as to the meaning of this offering by saying that these puja things were foundation-laying ritual objects for the grand fort the Emperor must now build on his land. Charming. Obsequious. Then there were gory tales of killings and betrayals. Of Salim's defiance of his father. Of Salim's great atelier of painters. Of the beheading of Akbar's favourite chronicler, Abul Fazl, and the secret place where the head lay, somewhere in the vast interiors of the Fort. This was more to the point, he thought, closer to the problem on hand. Histories still more brutal, alongside a serene watercolour of dawn lighting up the drawbridge. How the five sons of the Nawab of Farrukhabad were walled up alive in some unknown chamber of the fort by Nawal Rai, the Diwan/Subedar, after he'd extracted a massive ransom from their mother, the Begum of Farrukhabad in return of a promise of release and safe conduct for them. He studied the painting of the drawbridge and read the story of a great flood when the waters of the Ganga and the Yamuna broke through the embankment and poured into the city and how the Subedar of the fort had the bridge drawn up leaving desperate citizens to drown, admitting only the ones who could pay him what he demanded. The corpses are what stayed rotting on treetops all around the fort, after the waters receded.

It all seemed to be a warming up exercise for his own confessions. The embankment raised as much as a protection from the fury of the rivers as from the predatory Marathas who rampaged into the city, burning and looting. The story of a disempowered Mughal Emperor brought for sanctuary into the fort, the mild man who sat in state, inspecting the levee in a painting, who wrote Braj verse with tender grace and who would later be blinded, when he left the fort and the city. He read of the revelry of drunken soldiers, raiding the cellars before riding off to shoot their officers. He turned another page and read of frightened British women and children huddled in the sweltering chambers of the fort in the stench of cholera vomit and the reek of festering wounds and stale blood, while guns boomed outside and the smell and smoke of burning bungalows rose above the riverside groves. The illustrations showed vivid flares of flame erupting into sooty skies, women in draggled hair and limp skirts bent, hands clasped in prayer, children tugging at their sleeves.

The book was a collectors' item to be treasured but as he turned the pages he ran into the same old dilemma. Between the sweat and gore, the reek of terror and the strangled howls of beastly torture and these serene, art-cooled pages, lay the same distance that lay between his plural truths. It was funny but he came to look on the Fort as an elder who might say— look how I dress it all up, look on my grand costumery. Still he felt fortified enough—he was too absorbed to notice the significance of that word—to take the plunge, to lift the pen, flick open the notebook, take a deep breath and fling himself into the eye of the storm, the 3rd of November, 1962, when he, Col Jayant Mittra had arrived at Tashigaon in Bhutan. Too difficult, writing of those days. As though a gap had opened in the ground and trapped them in a bowel of experience unutterable in the speech of men. A sick blur of confused reflexes, frantic ruses and desperate choices that somehow just about managed to work out. In later years everything resisted the recall of those appalling images.

To other people, sheltered away somewhere in a normal

world, those days had not dropped out of the calendar. Exactly what had happened? His mind reached back and groped in the wreckage. There had been no time to lift them as they fell, those comrades of old, no residual sense to spare for those cries. The ones that fell were left behind alone in the snow, their voices beaten down by the rattle and boom of gunfire.

But he had it all in the wrong sequence. It had come to him as a shock that his GOC had proceeded on leave. But then it was rumoured those days that anybody who protested was removed, sacked or overruled, and this the old man couldn't possibly have taken. He had fathered the battalion for a long period and every one of them, officers, JCOs and troops, knew of the old man's obstinacy. On the afternoon of October 20th, the wireless set broke down. Fifteen days. It felt like an age. Time had stretched to its ultimate scope, like a high tension wire twanging taut. What was remarkable was that, dangerously close to snapping as it had been, some fine pliancy of fibre had not given way. Tired, hungry, sick, cold, scarcely human, they had found themselves in Bhutan, miraculously alive.

On the 20th of October he had spoken to the General at 1045 hours, when all seemed over and 7 Brigade no more. He had then started the withdrawal from Bridge 2 to Hathung-La at 1130 hours.

The intensity of the Chinese firing increased and they began shelling the position at about 1200 hours. He had closed down the wireless set at 1245 hours and under heavy enemy fire withdrawn in the direction of Hathung-La. Close on his heels pelted the Chinese for about two and a half hours and turned abruptly towards a feature south of Bridge 2 rather than Hathung-La. There was just a single thought pulsing in his hyperactive brain—to communicate somehow with the General and give him the gist of the situation. He still nursed a vague hope that there in that real world of order and sense there were people who would be able to grasp the horror of the situation and who still held the power to reverse it.

But as he headed in desperate haste towards that feature south of Hathung-La, the 62 wireless set that he was carrying had slipped from his hands and crashed to its doom and the wireless had gone mute. There was now no possibility of contact either with Tezpur or with their rear at Lumpu. For all intents and purposes they had stepped over the rim of the normal world, out of the range of human reach and recall. This is where it all ends, he had thought. What happens now shall never be known to anybody in that other retreated world. Now we stagger on, taking cover, blundering forward with only a confused instinct to guide us.

On the morning of the 21st they were shelled again and encircled. This fire came from a position well towards the south of Tsangdhar towards Karpola. And when they reached Hathung-La at last, the Chinese were there. Thousands of them, or so it had seemed. Turning back in haste, they withdrew. The night was spent some distance above the pass with the enemy only three or four hundred yards away. There was only one thing for it—to head for the Sherkham Nilaya area. Suddenly they had come across some leftover troops of the 4 Grenadiers. And just as suddenly they had found themselves encircled and under heavy fire.

They were crossing tortuous terrain, trackless jungle spawned wild across precipitous hills. With the greatest effort, dragging their blistered feet, they had gained a position west of a lone hut south of Hathung-La by the evening of the 22nd. On the 23rd it had been another desperate climb towards Lumpu, moving slowly west of the Lumpu ridge. Suddenly from that vantage point they had seen with a sharp pang that that the Chinese had occupied Lumpu too. On the 24th there was a near ambush when the Chinese spotted and shelled them intensively. The column had broken up. The night was spent in the dense jungle. In the concentrated blackness the jungle had been hell and haven both, swarming with horrors where torture or death might claim one from any undreamt-of quarter.

At first light they were up, the jungle mysteriously stirring around them. Now it had to be Tawang. Walking all day, they had crossed the Tsangdhar-Lumpu track at 1400 hours on the 25th of October. Here they had again been encircled and a prodigious amount of gunfire had rained down on them from the distant Lumpu zone. Struggling, hounded, and at the end of their tether, they had stumbled to the north of Shakti on their way to Tawang. That night they heard over a small transistor radio that the Indian army had vacated Tawang and the Chinese had moved in. He never knew what it was that had kept them going. Just the obscure knowledge that when there could be no turning back, the only option was to go on or else drop down dead. And they did not drop down dead.

Early in the morning of the 26th they climbed the steep Yamla mountain, 17,500 feet high. A half-melted moon faded slowly out of the sky. The night was spent under very heavy snow. There was no question of moving the boys any further that day. They had lain down in their summer uniforms, huddled beneath their single blankets.

After that came a large blank in memory, the mind revolting and refusing to register any ordered impressions. A kind of troubled sleep of the senses took over in which the limbs kept plodding in automaton precision and the insensate mind moved in a limbo of consciousness. When lucid images awoke in his mind again he grasped the fact that, cutting their own track through thick, wooded slopes, they had at last found themselves at Sulmang on the 29th of October.

None of them had had a bite to eat for nine whole days. At Sulmang they were able to buy some makki from the villagers. Then they trudged along a village track, passing settlements and sympathetic and hospitable villages, until they reached Tashigaon in Bhutan. Looking back on those nine days, the Chinese had seemed everywhere. All those passes—Kiya-La, Poshing-La, Hathung-La, were occupied. If they reached a pass, the Chinese had bombarded them with mortars from above. The enemy had used bird calls to signal to one another. Some of them had even donned Indian uniforms, taken off the bodies of Indian corpses, and barked out confusing orders. Marches there had been and counter-marches. The jungles, the hills were crawling with them. The rattle of automatic rifles sounded, like the snap and crackle of lightning from several directions, remote or close at hand, until it was like fighting an invisible enemy. There had been sudden, sinister lulls when only the wind soughed through the thick growth, ploughing through high walls of trees, snarling down the echoing hollows, and they found themselves alone in the suspense of a temporary respite.

The outlaws of the region had been on the Chinese side.

Silver coins had been dealt out and lists of the poor prepared. Endless propaganda had been carried out and guileful appeals. Standing on the Yamla summit, he recovered that bitter grief of personal failure that the gunfire had numbed and his mind, awake once more, had sought to retrace the panic and pain of a particular monstrous morning. A twenty-to-one chance they had had. In their cotton uniforms, without air or artillery support and rifle ammunition to last them just about half an hour, they had held their twelve-mile line of defence, certain of disaster, standing their ground, fighting to the last man and the last round. In four hours they were decimated, falling one by one, calculating every flimsy chance, estimating the moment and going wrong. There were a thousand ways to get it wrong. And those others got it wrong. He wasn't one of them, he scarcely understood how or why. Then they'd found themselves in the wilds with that carnage left behind them.

At Hathung-La the Chinese had taken a few prisoners on the 21st and the 22nd of October and shot some of them. Injured soldiers were tied to jeeps and dragged down the hilly roads and their brains battered to shreds.

It was only now that those dreadful images broke loose in his brain, phantoms held so long at bay, and a terrible rigour shook him all over and all the violent horror and recoil of days made his mouth go dry and an unuttered shout of rage strain and pull at the muscles of his throat. Gory visions pursued him. Of the brave, wounded Sikhs tied to Chinese jeeps, being dragged down the rocky roads, their flesh tearing, strangled animal cries breaking out of mangled lips until his heart grew sick and faint at the memory and a convulsive shudder overpowered him.

There were things he had not told the General. How the twelve of them had staggered in the jungle for days, weak with hunger, running high fever, delirious and hallucinating. After all the intervening years he still hoped that ultimate horror was something they had hallucinated. How each one had secretly wished that one of the twelve would drop down dead and his body provide food for the surviving seven. How murder had crept into the hearts of old mates and they grew suspicious of one another, ravenous like beasts in the wilds. A mouse had been felled with a belt and a savage brawl had broken out to claim its raw, scanty flesh. The body of the mouse, stripped to the bone, was an image that refused to go away—and the body of the man who fought like the devil to seize the mouse and gnaw at it before anyone else could. Who suddenly lay dead, eyes still staring at the mouse held tightly in his fist, from which someone prised it out. He still remembered the man's face, every detail of it, a reedy, slight man with a wheezy cough and a face yellow with starvation. His stomach turned and his conscious mind fought to expunge that particular thought. He still wasn't sure he'd killed that man, though his companions claimed he had.

When, hours or days afterwards, the helicopters were sighted, they had crawled forwards on their bellies and somehow managed to light a fire—and sent up a smoke signal. A blurred memory surfaced, how they had leapt on the sacks of rice that the helicopters dropped and with what brutish hunger they had fallen on them. Stuffing the hard, uncooked grains of rice by the handful into dry, gnawing mouths. A few hours later, death, which had spared them when they were most famished, came to lay its claim on four sick men, groaning from the agony burning in their bellies and the blood boiling out of their bowels, the uncooked rice completing the cycle of starvation that had lasted many days.

A man shot dead over a mouse—this was no heroic tale. Shabby it was and sordid, low, shaming, vile. He had only to lower the drawbridge of his mind and all the ghastly, mocking visions came pouring in. There were atrocities of grander scale, indignities too. Things that did not fill a man with the sort of foul loathing that overcame him when he recalled these, as though the stench of shame had come to stay and choke his breath and all that he honoured of himself had rotted away to a filthy, squelching, stomach-turning mulch of odium.

He had got it all down on paper, the fetid disgorged mess of his mind, and suddenly he came to himself, trembling, his collar wet with perspiration despite the air conditioning. The room felt close and his breath came short.

In a daze he picked up the book again and it fell open to a random page. His eye paused on a photograph. A tall pillar, the light leading the eye upwards along its vertical shaft. Severe and solitary, like the forefinger of an explicating sage. Covered with fine inscriptions, an old encoded script of hard-earned enlightenment. But of course, this was Ashoka, who else would know his own situation better? Reading, he found himself in fellowship with a king who'd recoiled from war and who probably had known his own share of Post-Traumatic Stress Disorder, even though it may have gone under a different name.

The Fifth Pillar Edict. Thus saith His Sacred and Gracious Majesty the King—After I had been consecrated twenty-six years the following species were declared exempt from slaughter, to wit:- Parrots, starlings, adjutants, Brahmani ducks, geese, Mandimukhas, geldatas, bats, queen ants, female tortoises, boneless fish, Vedaveyakas, Ganga puputakas, tortoises, porcupines, tree squirrels, deer, Barasinghas, Brahmini bulls, monkeys, rhinocerii, grey doves, village pigeons and all four-footed animals which are not utilized or eaten. She-goats, ewes, and sows, that is to say, those either with young or in milk, are exempt from slaughter, as well as their offspring up to six months of age. The caponing of cocks must not be done. Chaff must not be burnt along with the living thing in it. Forests must not be burnt, either for mischief or so as to destroy life. The living must not be fed with the living.

'At each of the three seasonal full moons, and at the full moon of the month of Tishya, for three days in each case, namely the fourteenth and fifteenth of the first fortnight, and the opening day of the second fortnight, as well as on the fastdays throughout the year, fish is exempt from killing and may not be sold. On the same days in elephant preserves and fish ponds no other classes of animals may be destroyed. On the eighth, fourteenth and fifteenth days of each fortnight as well as on the Tishya and Punarvasu days, on the three seasonal full moon days and on festival days bulls must not be castrated, and he-goats, rams, boars or other animals which are commonly castrated must not be castrated. On the Tishya and Punarvasu days, on the seasoned full-moon days, and during the seasonal full moon fortnights, the branding of horses and oxen must not be done...'

It was hardly the sort of thing to be expected in the heart of a citadel of war, the sort of thought a hardened warrior might entertain. Yet there it was, comprehensive in its concern, passionate, unashamed in its unmartial mercy. Spreading the ample fold of its sheltering protection on all sentience. As though that hoary elder, the Allahabad Fort, that old war veteran, had pronounced—there is this too, here within these walls, and to have known one register of reality is not to abdicate another. It's all here, jumbled together, so sleep in peace.

SEVEN

The Last Telegram of Allahabad

⟡

What a rage he'd been in the seventies, a rockstar of a teacher. Anita remembered how she'd reach early to class to be able to sit in the front bench, right beneath the wooden rostrum of the teacher's desk. He in his late twenties, she fresh out of school and all of eighteen years. They'd grown up in adjacent bungalows on Clive Road but when she was playing with her doll's tea-set out on the lawn of her house, he'd been practising riding round on a friend's Lambretta scooter and neither had noticed the other. But when she joined her B.A., he'd been away for some years, had returned and was already teaching. Looking back, she'd have sworn that right from the very first week, their eyes had marked each other down as the one.

The class had noticed. 'Today sir only taught you!'—the girl students pulled her leg while the boys grew wary of her. Only once had she tried to sit in one of the back benches. And that had been because she'd brought along a small battery-operated tape recorder to record his lecture in secret, to be able to hear his voice again and again in the privacy of her room, but he'd thwarted the attempt, to their mutual embarrassment, to their mutual benefit, as it turned out. 'Where is Anita Chandra today?'—he'd searched the crowd of heads in something like dismay. 'Is she absent? Oh there you are. What are you doing in that last row, if I may ask?' She'd stood up. The tape recorder an awkward bulk weighing down her shoulder bag. 'Anita is recording your voice, sir!' called out her friend, Geeta. He'd stared at her in shock that turned into feigned amusement. 'Bring that thing here, please.' His voice was peremptory. She'd carried the thing up to the teacher's desk. Neither of them had known how best to translate this into a classroom joke.

'You were going to record my lecture?'

'Yes, sir, it...it saves time.'

'Very practical, I must say,' he'd started laughing.

'Okay,' he'd said. 'Have it your own way. Switch it on.' She'd obeyed.

He'd put on a special discursive voice and launched forth: 'Given the existence as uttered forth in the public works of Puncher and Wattmann of a personal God quaquaquaqua with white beard quaquaquaqua outside time without extension who from the heights of divine apathia divine athambia divine aphasia loves us dearly with some exceptions for reasons unknown but time will tell and suffers like the divine Miranda with those who for reasons unknown but time will tell are plunged in torment plunged in fire whose fire flames if that continues and who can doubt it will fire the firmament that is to say blast hell to heaven so blue still and calm so calm which even though intermittent is better than nothing but not so fast and considering what is more that as a result of the labours left unfinished crowned by the Acacacacademy of

Anthropopopopometry of Essy-in-Possy of Testew and Cunard it is established beyond all doubt all other doubt than that which clings to the labours of men...'

He spoke from memory, modulating his classroom voice, now exaggeratedly declaiming, now sweetly reasonable, now thunderous, now appealing, steering his voice through the whole scale of vocal possibilities till the class was helpless with laughter and he reached forward and pressed the switch-off button of the tape recorder.

'Do not, for one moment imagine that I made this up,' he smiled. 'If you open your books to page 43, you shall find an exact transcript of my recent lecture. In fact, you'll find it goes on for two whole pages. That's Becket at his best. Lucky's speech in your *Waiting For Godot*. And what do you think it means? Before I launch into literary criticism, I want you to write out an interpretation of this for the next seminar class. Meanwhile I shall deviate from what I planned to teach today. Instead I shall speak on a subject I enjoy—Abracadabra in literature and philosophy.' Then he'd spoken of the Buddha's speech, of the breakdown of language, of meanings held in webs of silence, of mantric tonalities, of syllabic adventures. Of Manto's 'Toba Tek Singh'. Of that new Les Murray poem he'd come across which was called 'Bats' Ultrasound' which went—and here he recited: 'ah, eyrie-ire, aero hour, eh? O'er our ur-area (our era aye ere, yaw raw row) we air our array, err, yaw, row wry—aura our orrery, our eerie u our ray, our arrow. A rare ear, our aery Yahweh.'

Thirty-seven years down the line, married to him, watching over his wheelchair, she felt herself go numb, thinking of his last, stubborn lectures in that very hall. The great stone hall with its lofty lintelled teak doors, its massive windows and its majestic ceiling had once boomed with the voices of Sir Tej Bahadur Sapru and Motilal Nehru and the legendary teachers of the University's English Department, Jha and Deb and Dustoor and Firaq and Bachchan, but never before had such a voice as his, risen in eloquent expression as now in a register of utterance enough to abash the hoary walls into stunned deference. His voice struggling desperately in incomprehensible squawks and jarring quavers, pushing against the paralysed vocal chords in obstinate defiance, speech skewed into primitive animal sounds indecipherable to the hundred-odd students who sat, heads bowed, quiet as mice, listening to the last heartbreaking strainings of their once-fluent professor. He'd sworn he'd be fine. He'd refused to go on leave, despite the urgings of his colleagues and research scholars. He'd fought against the idea of a wheelchair.

That day, cleaning out a cupboard, Anita came across that old cassette. On an impulse she switched on the antique tape recorder, snapped open its deck and slipped in that cassette. She didn't know whether she was disappointed or relieved when the ribbon stuck in the cogs and the wheels jammed still, and she rescued the remains of that long lost memory in a snarled mess of unspooled tape. To her gauche fingers it felt like time slipping out of its circuit, a tangled, uncontainable whorl.

That was what she seemed to be doing, much of the time. Retrieving days, events, and reliving them aloud for him, now that speech had left him, now that he sat in the wheelchair, his face locked in an immovable mask, and only his eyes alive, so alive, they burned into her face sometimes and she had to look away. It was a mercy that he could still write and write he did—in notebooks she bought for him from the students' bookstores on University Road, notebooks made of recycled paper, sold by the weight. And how he wrote—his hand gripping the ADD gel pen, tearing across the sheets in a sprawling script ravenous for the white page, ferociously mowing it down, demolishing the stillness creeping upon them both when his hands too would freeze, immobile. There were times when he seemed to be scribbling urgent memoranda to self but when she checked she found it to be mismatched lines from the old courses he used to teach at the University's English Department: 'Do not go gentle into that good night, rage, rage against the dying of the light.' He wrote the word 'rage', then the word 'rave', then crossed out the latter. Or on another day: 'Thou art indeed just Lord if I contend with Thee.' He'd had problems with the word 'contend' and had followed it up with 'pretend'. He used to write the same line over and over again as though he were teaching his hand to memorize the movement on the paper. Hundreds of times in the old days she'd urged him: 'You must write, Mrinal. You must stop your chattering and write it down. You have a hundred books in you!' He'd always said: 'I know, I know. One of these days I'll get down to it.' Now he wrote, wrote and wrote, a lot of it undecipherable, his handwriting going fast. But, as it happened, all his black humour intact, flashing forth like a whiplash streaking through the air. This is my MS, he once wrote, and did not relent even when she broke down, only added two more words to his tempestuous scrawl: Dramatic irony.

Still, it was his dark humour that kept him going, his very cussedness. She read out the most provocative bits of

news from the paper each morning, glad to ignite political
rage, social contempt, scoffing laughter, anything to keep this
healthy, holy anger alive. The newspaper hour always started
with the date, the month. It was important to spell that out.

'It's the 13th of July. And guess what, tomorrow it's
going to be farewell to the telegram forever. Like the steam
engine, telegrams will be museum things, she told him. D'you
remember how you used to declare your love for me in telegram
messages?'

His eyes smiled behind his mask.

'The boys at the telegraph office desk made such hilarious
howlers—can't blame them. They weren't expected to know
your upper-crust Eng-Lit. And I was in splits when telegrams
from you mis-quoted everything with a vengeance. Oh, how
come I've never told you this one?'

The telegram, one of his early ones, read:

Drink to me only with thine eyes
And I will pledge with mine STOP
Or leave a piss but in the cup and I'll not look for wine
STOP

His eyes were convulsed with laughter.

'How could I have forgotten to tell you?' She laughed. 'Oh,
I know. We girls in the Department were so very Victorian
those days. So propah, so decorous in our sarees and long
braids and chignons. How could we utter a word like "piss" to
a poetic admirer! Good girls never pissed. If you mentioned
any such low function we'd probably scream and call out for
our smelling salts, after the Brontë and Jane Austen heroines
we read about. Ah, those days.'

Suddenly it was terrifically important to communicate every tiny fragment of unshared memory with him. One of the incidental fears of her situation was that something would be left unshared, that some trivialia, some detail, might surface that she'd have to live with alone in the long years ahead. The newspaper coverage in the two papers they subscribed to obviously kept him interested and she chose bits and pieces of special interest.

'It says here that once a telegram arrived from Calcutta with the message: "Bengali sweets despatched" and it threw the Viceroy's security establishment in Shimla into a tizzy because in those days of the freedom struggle Bengali sweets was a code for bombs. What actually happened was that someone called Sir Chettur Sankaran Nair who was a member of the Viceroy's council had invited the Viceroy to dinner at his bungalow named Inverarm in Shimla and he thought of serving rasgullas and sent for them all the way from Calcutta—but the entire police department was thrown into a flutter and the rasgullas and the telegram were delivered only after thorough investigations had been made. Funny, isn't this?'

He had heard her with an interested look in his eyes, as he did when she read out the paper to him. She combed the paper for more anecdotes. 'It says here that the shortest telegram in the world was just a question mark—see here—a "?"' She showed him the paper. 'It was sent by Oscar Wilde to his publisher asking how his new book was faring. And the publisher's reply by telegram was no less short. It was an exclamation mark—an "!" Enough to convey the general idea that sales were roaring ahead.'

If he could smile, he would have. This was the sort of

anecdotal thing he loved hearing.

'The longest telegram was 175 pages long—the entire text of the Nevada State Constitution, sent to Abraham Lincoln by wire in 1864! It makes me think of all those long letters you used to send me by wire—what a torment they must have been for the cable guys tapping brass on brass in the instrument room of the telegraph office. And when the khaki-clad telegram man arrived on his bicycle, first thing my mother threw a fit. Because the telegram man meant someone's illness, someone's death or someone's unwelcome arrival. I used to slink into my room and wait for my father to come thundering in, waving the pink telegram in the air with a look of such disgust. Those pretty pink sheets with the type-written words pasted on, remember? Two kinds, ordinary and express. And those special ones with a band of colourful lotuses and bells. I used to go to the telegraph office to reply to your telegrams and the fellows there used to smirk at my cryptic messages. And then there was the phonogram. I can rattle off the alphabet codes still—A for army, D for doctor, E for English, L for lady, C for cinema. Even the numbers for those standard messages. 5 for many happy returns of the day, 21 for wishing the function every success, 25 for may heavens rain choicest blessings on the young couple...'

He signalled that he wanted to write something by way of comment. She gave him the notebook, put the pen between his thumb and forefinger. He wrote carefully: '100 for condolences.'

She looked at him, pained, puzzled. 'Why this?' she wanted to know. More black humour?

He began writing again. She could not read his fixed face

but she had learnt to interpret the expressions of his writing hand, the tension of his wrist, the pressure of nib on paper, sometimes so fierce that the rough, recycled paper tore under the pen, stabbed to the hilt. She read: STOP.

She stopped, stricken. 'Does this upset you—talking about the past?'

He wrote: 'Fuck the past.'

She grew confused. 'I'm sorry,' she said. 'I won't do it.'

But he was unsparing. 'The fucking past is all I have and no fucking future do you have to fucking rub it in.'

His mood swings. There were times when his hand acquired a manic life of its own and stormed across the sheets of the notebook, abusing, cursing. Their son, their daughter-in-law, his friends, his colleagues. His pen disgorged venom and she let him. Later she tried to soothe him. Don't blame the poor boy, she'd counsel. It is the way of life. A son is a son till he gets a wife and a daughter is a daughter for life—remember that old saying. It is too bad we have no daughter. Don't hold it against the boy. Don't blame Siddhartha either—he didn't know you're touchy about those things. He meant well—and he comes every bloody day to see you. Don't look at me like that. It's you he comes to see, not me. I wish you'd get over this old foolishness of yours. Don't be so mad at poor Ranjit. He doesn't mean to hurt you when he lifts you out of your chair. He's just too full of beans—a lad of twenty-two, what d'you expect?' Lately his writing had grown laboured, the words askew and the thoughts more basic—food, sleep, bowel movements. It was roughly the time when the diapers had become necessary.

On the 18th of February she'd had a party for him.

Invited all their friends, ostensibly to celebrate his birthday, had a cake with fifty-nine candles and all. It was a sunny winter morning, cool and breezy, the air like polished glass, and they'd gathered on the lawn for the birthday brunch, as they used to do long ago. The winter flowers a riot of colour, the roses in full bloom, the cane and rattan chairs sparkling white or polished walnut, the garden umbrellas pretty in the mid-morning sun, the grass fluorescent green. She wanted him to meet everyone possible, friends, relatives, old servants. Gone to great lengths. For a few hours it felt as though time had changed tack. That they were back in the sixties and his father's old Buick and Graham Page were still parked in the portico, gleaming under old Bhoora Singh, the driver's care. That Father's old hookah-bearer stood ready to take the hats and hang them neatly on the old teak hat-stand. The front lawns rang with laughter, the side orchards stood laden with fruits—limes, grapefruits, guavas, bananas. The two old bulls, yoked to a wooden device that worked the pulley on the transverse beam of the well, going round and round, drawing up endless supplies of water for the garden, and the malis sprinkling the broad, curved driveway with water to keep the dust down and the air fragrant. The bearer boys flitted about with trays of drinks and savouries and through the massive arching teak doors of the bungalow one could see the Barrister-Sahib's majestic library behind his imposing teak desk and the heavy swivelling bookshelf.

Only now the guests were dressed far more casually. The slender women with flowers in their hair and crepe or georgette sarees draped round their lissom forms were now solidly obese or scrawny-slim and dressed in churidars and kurtas and trousers and kurtis, the men who used to be in formal wear were in T-shirts and jeans. But the laughter hadn't changed, and the back-slapping, the leg-pulling, the jokes which were inlaid with cross-references and obscurities that everyone knew everything about—if anything grown more self-consciously uproarious and the old nick-names sounded just as chummy, just as teasing—Monty and Tubbles and Dotty and Sandwich and Kitkitiya. Most lived in houses like her own—with lawns well kept or gone to seed, with vast outhouses of former servants and their teeming descendants behind the imperious tiled bungalows. Anita had invited their old servants too.

'Do you recognize him?' she asked him, steering a shrunken old man with caved jowls up to the wheelchair. 'He's Pukkun, our Ayah's son.'

'Remember Pukkun?—he'd been brought in as a playmate and companion for you. Those playmates who lived in thatched huts at the rear end of the grounds, who held the kites aloft or ran to catch the straying ball, who spun the tops with you or dug the marbles out of holes or played chequers with polished tamarind seeds. Who later talked girls and even, who knows, became partners in in-house secrecies.'

Yes, of course, Pukkun. His eyes remembered Pukkun.

'What are you doing now, Pukkun?'

'Nothing much, Baby,' said the old fellow. Yes, it was still Baby or Baba. One old man addressing another one as Baba or calling an old lady Baby was nothing to wonder at! 'I live with my second son, the one who is a P.C.S. in Pratapgarh!'

'Oh, great! Did you hear that, Mrinal? Pukkun's son is a P.C.S. officer. And our old driver's daughter, I learnt the other day, is an engineer!'

'Pukkun's done very well for himself,' was the general verdict.

'So has Gopal's daughter,' Tubbles volunteered the information. 'She's an engineer from an I.I.T. Imagine!'

'Oh, Gopal was our ace bowler. There used to be cricket matches between the bungalows. Teams made up of the boys of the family, even the young juniors of barristers, and, with absolute democracy, the boys from the outhouses of rival bungalows. 'Gopal was our hero,' recalled Tubbles. 'He always made our bungalow win against Mishraji's bungalow. Of course, he never touched us. He scrupulously avoided us. And when our team won and we howled for joy and hugged one another, Gopal shouted and sang for joy all by himself, touching no one.'

'And this is Imtiaz, our old darzi, Wahid Mian's son,' she introduced the tall, stooped, bearded man in the faded safari suit. 'Wahid Mian used to sit cross-legged in the inner verandah, turning out frocks and skirts and blouses for my sister-in-law. I wasn't an inmate, of course, but I was a frequent visitor, being almost family. And what a storyteller, was Wahid Mian, and what a clown. He'd juggle his shoulders up and down, his round spectacles sliding down his pudgy nose, and sing jingles for the kids of the house. Then at noon he'd solemnly offer namaz, graciously accept the lunch offered and lie curled up on his mat for a while. At three in the afternoon the sewing machine would be whirring again.' But Mrinal's face stayed blank. Wahid Mian had faded, as had so many of those other family retainers, the scolding supervisors of meals, the philosophers of rustic wisdom, the discreet eavesdroppers, the surreptitious counsellors.

'Imtiaz's son Zahid is free these days. He'll be coming to help Ranjit look after you.' She made it sound like a special present, a birthday surprise. A surprise he didn't register, though everyone else stopped chattering for a second. She spoke fast, covering up the dire reality of the need for two men now to lift and assist. 'Imtiaz used to be our vegetable vendor and he used to bring his cartful of veggies to our courtyard gate and sing for us. Such funny things. "Laila ki unglian, majnoon ki paslian!" For bhindis from his fields near the Yamuna. And such a melodious singer—Uncle used to say to him—Son, what the hell are you doing, selling vegetables? You should be training at the Prayag Sangeet Samiti.'

'Sing us a few of those, Imtiaz,' begged one of the guests. 'Haven't heard a real old-world singing hawker for a long time, makes my head go tipsy with nostalgia!'

Imtiaz blushed, hung his head, 'Arey, you are joking, Baba,' he told the snowy-haired visitor.

'I swear I'm not,' insisted the other. 'No better music for me.'

But Imtiaz wouldn't oblige.

'Tell us the words then,' pleaded Anita. So Imtiaz hung his head and recited in a halting, embarrassed voice:

'Kya pyaari-pyaari meethhi aur patli-patliyan hain,
Ganne ki poriyan hain, resham ki takhliyan hain,
Farhad ki nigaahein, Sheereen ki hansliyan hain,
Majnu ki sard aahein, Laila ki unglian hain,
Kya khoob narmo-nazuk, yeh Ilahabad ki kakriyan hain…'
Great applause greeted his dead-pan recital.

'Wonderful, Imtiaz! And I wish you'd sung it out as you used to.'

'Actually, that's a nazm by Nazir Akbarabadi,' said Tubbles, the shair. 'And Habib Tanvir has used it in his play *Agra Bazaar*. Our Ilahabadi hawkers have cleverly changed "Agra ki kakriyan" to "Ilahabad ki kakriyan".'

'Trust us Ilahabadis!'

'Someone also added that crazy line "Majnu ki pasliyan!"'

'What would that be?'

'The ribs of Majnu.'

'Ingenious.'

Only Mrinal sat stony-faced, apparently comprehending nothing. It was then that the shocking suspicion dawned in Anita's mind that Mrinal's mind had disowned the past. That he was present and not present.

'Now, for the best part of the day,' she clapped and announced. 'I have actually succeeded in persuading Mrinal to sit at the piano again and play us something. Yes, really. If you all step into the drawing room…'

The wheelchair was drawn up in front of the grand piano, his hands lifted and placed on the keyboard. He looked long at the keyboard with interest, acknowledging its familiarity. Then his fingers moved, as they did across the pages of the notebook, moved and faltered. But Anita had thought of that in advance. From the huge old radiogram-cum-tape deck swung out the joyous strains of 'Eine Kleine Nachtmusique' and Mrinal gazed at his limp hands with amazement in his eyes, as he let them trail in the stream of glittering notes that lapped at his fingertips like tiny, shining fish. It was her special gift to him—to let him feel the music as though he were playing it himself. The guests sat in a pin-drop silence, suddenly sober despite the vodka. Mrinal sat with eyes closed, his faintly quivering fingers lapsed languorous on the keys as though the keyboard was a living, beloved, comforting thing. When the piece ended his hands fell asleep on the black and ivory keys in such pitiful surrender that one of his college buddies, Ditto, was moved to exclaim: Go on, Mrinal boy. Play us another one. Yes, Mrinal, this was splendid. We've never heard you play this well, cried Jinny. Play us that one you used to play at Clareton College—what was it called?—It was what we called The Moony Sonata. Why the Moony Sonata? Abhyuday wanted to know. Those days he was mooning over Sabby, remember? Do you have the Moonlight Sonata, Anita?

Oh, sure. She had quickly looked through her stack of records and found it. She had noticed that at the very mention of that name Mrinal had opened his eyes. To close them again as the memory of the music softly drifted past his fingertips. Sabby. Sabrina. The 'Facebook Flame', as she and Mrinal used to call her not so very long ago, while he could still speak. Mooning over Sabby? Anita's head was in a whirl. Hadn't he told her he had never met this Sabrina? That she was just someone he met in an internet chat-room? Clareton College? That was thirty-odd years ago, while he'd been a student. Mooning over…the full import of it struck her suddenly and all she could do was work hard to keep her face in check and her voice under control.

That evening she asked him in a carefully casual voice: 'This Sabby and Sabrina are the same, Mrinal?' He did not answer. She repeated her question. She hoped he'd write something, explain, but he didn't seem to register her question at all. Was it cruel to badger him like that? Better to let it go. That was quite some while back.

So when the phone rang in the sitting room that July morning and their old bearer, Vishnu, picked it up and came into the verandah to tell them: 'It's for you Baby,' she was quite unprepared for the melodious voice that came across the line. 'Is that Anita? Hullo, Anita. This is Sabrina Sinha.'

'Yes?' she responded, finding it hard to speak steadily.

'You might not know me. In fact I'm pretty sure you don't. I'm an old friend of Mrinal's—classmate at Clareton. Heard he was poorly from Dotty Dasgupta—Devendra Dasgupta— do you know Devendra Dasgupta?' The voice was soft and springy, with a kind of jaunty energy.

'Yes, of course I know Dotty,' Anita answered.

'I'm here in connection with a case in the High Court— I'm a rights lawyer—and when Dotty told me about what's happened to Mrinal, I said to myself, "I really must drop in and see him when I'm in Allahabad."'

'You're welcome,' Anita answered in a voice that bordered on coolness. She tried to cover it up with a contrived rush of bright enthusiasm. 'Mrinal's told me about you, so even if I've never actually met you, I've known you a long while. Yes, please do come. Any time…'

'Six o'clock suits you?' The voice at the other end seemed a bit off-colour but she may have been imagining it.

'Perfect,' she heard her own voice utter an abnormal lilt. 'Be expecting you then.'

She didn't quite know what made her ask Ranjit, their grown-up attendant 'boy': 'Any phone calls today, Ranjit?'

She was hardly surprised when he answered, 'Ji, memsahib. There was a call for Sahib but it came on the mobile. It was a madam. She said to hold the phoon to Sahib's ear…'

He was a canny one, this Ranjit, and good at innuendoes although he kept his face innocent.

When she came into Mrinal's room at five-thirty in the evening, dressed in her new chiffon kurta of pastel dove-grey, she sniffed: 'What's this strange new smell, Ranjit?'

He used to attend to Mrinal's needs when she was away at the bank or the market or the insurance offices that covered his mediclaim or the private interviews with his doctor.

'Sahib wanted deeo, memsahib. Sahib want clean shirt.'

'I see,' she remarked, wondering how Sahib indicated these things to Ranjit, then she caught sight of the crumpled paper in the waste-paper basket and, under the pretext of fixing the buckle of her sandal, bent and fished it out. She took it out to the sitting room and smoothed it out on the side table. There was a single word on it—DeeO. Surely Ranjit could decode it. What's going on here? She stumbled into the sofa thinking. And what's the matter with me? Should she ask Ranjit if he bought the cologne for Mrinal while she was away and how. 'Telephoned the chemist, Sahib's Protinex was due today and the physiotherapist picked it up, memsahib,' was Ranjit's expressionless answer. She had to carefully adjust her face in a jokey playfulness, then she wondered which shirt Mrinal had wanted to wear. She went in again to check and found it to be exactly the one she'd expected, a fine sea-green lawn shirt that had been a favourite with him. It was an effort to keep herself from remarking on it. There were still some minutes left.

'I've sent for some special chocolate cookies,' she engaged herself in bright, busy chatter with him. 'And also some of those pista burfis you like. Then I wondered what namkeens I should arrange. Would samosas be too hot and greasy for your stylish friend—I'm sure she's stylish, being your friend. I settled for dhoklas from Kamdhenu and sandwiches and cheese puffs. Sure that's all right? I'll give her a choice between fresh juice or coffee. Oh well, maybe, you'll want champagne!' There was this strange pitch to her voice, edgy, almost shrill that she was sure he noticed. He was that sensitive to tones. But he wasn't paying attention. He sat still and it dawned on her that he was listening intently. For what? Definitely not her natter. For the crunch of car wheels on the gravel? For the sound of a familiar step? Really, she scolded herself, I've got to stop this. But she did run down the corridor to her dressing room, unlock her cupboard, take out her large diamond solitaire ring that he'd given her on their silver wedding, and slipped it on her finger before hurrying back to his room. They waited. For hours it seemed, although it was only about twenty minutes or so. Then the slam of a car door made her start up and she rose from her chair and went out into the verandah and the portico to meet Sabrina Sabby.

It was her voice that she heard first. Refined, poised, graceful. Saying to the chauffeur in delicate, anglicized Hindi: 'Thank you, thank you. I suppose I'll stay an hour here. Aap jaiye, kuch chai-pani kar aiye. Main phone se bula loongi.'

Anita stepped forward: 'Not at all necessary. Chai-pani here is all on the house!' It seemed a feeble sort of a quip, even a bit shabbily homey, but it sounded a strong, decisive welcome—far from what she felt. Heart sinking, she took in the splendid spectacle of the charismatic Sabrina Sinha as she emerged from the car. Stylish, had she jibed at Mrinal? She out-styled style itself! She might have been a style icon for those in their late fifties. Fitted black lycra pants, white linen pleated shirt, high heeled sandals, copper-varnished toe-nails. Hair swinging loose and perfectly tinted, somewhere between brown and burgundy. She carried a large suede shoulder bag, had a pair of white-framed sunglasses pushed up her forehead.

'He told me he was marrying a student.' The voice held a fine thread of amusement. 'I imagined someone young.'

'I guess, thirty years back you could call me that,' laughed Anita, resenting this.

'My mistake entirely.'

Sabrina Sabby was tall. She towered over Anita with the easy languor of one made for walking ramps. She shrugged with the air of a fashionista swinging a cape. 'We've all gotten on, grown old and weary and lined…' She laughed, a rich fruity laugh, as though she didn't believe a word of what she said.

'I have, not you,' said Anita, being winning, being noble.

'Get your eyes checked,' said Sabrina, 'in case you can't see my philosopher's frown and my laughter lines.'

'If you can laugh, you must be one—a philosopher, I mean,' rejoined Anita, congratulating herself on her own repartee. 'Do come in. He's in the sitting room. It's this way, to the right.'

'I know,' was Sabrina's easy answer, as she walked in, leading the way, leaving Anita wondering even more than before. She watched Sabrina enter the room and stand stock still a moment. She saw her readjust the bag on her shoulder and the look on her face and the words on her lips. But she was far more mindful of Mrinal's wooden face, his opaque eyes that gave nothing away, registered nothing.

'Here's Sabrina,' she stepped forward, pulling up a chair beside Mrinal for the guest to sit, pulling up another for herself, strategically placing it where she could study both their faces. She saw Sabrina sink into her chair in a sort of shock, her eyes on Mrinal. She saw Mrinal sit there, passive, expressionless.

The guest seemed momentarily at a loss for words. Uncharacteristically quiet. When she spoke her voice was faintly tuneless, deprived of its fine finish.

'Just look at you, man,' was what she said. The way she whispered the words to herself, she might have been talking to him in her head—or in some accustomed closeness in which neither needed to speak louder. Anita saw Mrinal's hands tighten—to know his reactions you had to watch his hands not his face—and that ever so slight tension of his fingers told her more than any tell-tale words or facial expressions could.

Sabrina reached forward and pushed a grey shock of hair off Mrinal's forehead. A gesture so personal, so intimate that it seemed an instinctive repetition of a practised movement unforgotten despite all the years.

'...so I kept one extra evening, in fact a day extra—because if I catch Kalka Mail tomorrow morning—it leaves at 9.30 and reaches Delhi in the evening, that's a day gone, but I couldn't not see you,' said Sabrina, as though picking up a conversation left unfinished. 'When Dotty rang me and gave me the details I rang up Subhash in New York and he made enquiries among all his fellow specialists...'

Who on earth was Subhash? What was she, single, married, divorced? Anita was suddenly incensed. For God's sake, drop that voice of pity, woman!—was what she wanted to scream. Instead she sat there, wearing her look of gentle wifely caring, self-effacing, obliging, ever accommodating.

'I hunted out this for you,' Sabrina announced, in what Anita found to be an insufferable baby-talking voice. Fairy godmother producing a gift! Patronizing nursie making the patient's day!

Sabrina had opened her suede bag and taken out a rectangular plastic packet. From its recesses she carefully produced an antique photo album, the kind people pasted their black-and-white photographs in. Leaves of stiff black, photos held in triangular corners, the binding a knotted silk tassel holding the thick, tapestried covers together.

'Can I have a table, please?' Sabrina turned and spoke to her as she might have spoken to a waiter or an inconsequential attendant.

'Oh, sure!'

Sabrina laid the album on the old card table that Anita had dragged up to the side of Mrinal's wheelchair.

'D'you recognize that bloke? Bimbo Banerjee, can you believe it? To look at him now you'd imagine he was eighty or something. I ran into him in London last year.'

She turned a page. 'I knew you'd enjoy this, Mika.'

Mika? Who was Bimbo Banerjee?

'That time we were all plain doped, so I can't ask you if you remember,' Sabrina was saying. 'The things you bastards did! At one of those jam sessions you guys filled up condoms and hung them up as balloons. I wasn't that keen on the joint as all the rest were so I have a pretty clear memory of you trying to be a lawnmower!'

She turned another page. 'Your Dad came storming in. Called his barber from the outhouse. Made him seize all you guys and give you all a drastic haircut. See how pathetic the lot of you look, all those fancy hippie looks gone! That short one in the corner is Bubbles Tandon, remember him? He was pretty broken, I tell you.'

Anita saw the pupils of Mrinal's eyes dance. Sabrina turned another page.

'That's the hell-and-thunder play we got together to write and perform. What was it called? Ah "The Storming of the Bastille". Bloody intense rubbish. What a coincidence—come to think of it, it's the 14th of July, tomorrow. Pretty weepy stuff. I was Marie Antoinette, remember? You were Pierre Charmont, the aristocrat. Ruchira Chatterjee was desperate for a part and tried hard to cadge one and there just weren't any roles left, so you said to her—"Say, Rummy, how d'you like to act the role of La Guillotine? All you do is come down like a ton of bricks on us—it's what you're so good at." She was that mad. She stopped coming to our rehearsals, she even stopped trailing you around...'

Another page: 'Our Garsarwa picnic. Can you recognize the group?'

Anita shifted uneasily in her chair. She felt an interloper. Clearly Mrinal had no objection to all this talk of the past and clearly that past had a lot of things and people he'd never told her about.

'That was the afternoon someone threw a stone at a massive bee-hive above the fall and the bees came swarming out in full battle mode and you pulled me into one of the caves so as to be out of their way.'

Anita rose softly to her feet. 'What would you like? Juice? Coffee?'

'Anything,' was Sabrina's answer. Anita realized she just

wasn't there with them in the room. 'Juice. No, coffee'd be fine.' Sabrina seemed to draw herself out of some sort of spell of shared memory and she turned to her and smiled a bright social smile in concession to her presence in the room.

She was glad to get away, she told herself, from that suffocating space. She'd need hours, days, to sort all this out in her agitated head. She'd have to work hard to convert the obvious into the acceptable and actually what was there to mind? As her hands worked, arranging the lace covers on the trolley and the starched napkins and the plates, and her lips moved in mechanical instructions to old Basant, their cook, her brain argued, reasoned, counselled, as best as it could. But what I object to, the thought broke loose from her battery of exonerations, is the lie, the lie. So unnecessary. Why ever did he need to lie? Unless there was something he held on to, something to protect from her prying, claiming love. There were sudden, sharp tears stinging her eyes and she didn't want Basant to see them so she pretended to drop a spoon on the counter and then wondered if he wondered why her hands shook. These outhouse servants were all-knowing and all-intuiting, she cursed. From Ranjit to Vishnu to Basant and probably to the entire huddle of huts that ran around the rear of their bungalow, the news must have travelled: Sahib's old girlfriend has arrived. Memsahib in a tizzy. Sabby knew her way about the house. Surely everyone here knew her or about her. Or were they laughing at her, their poor memsahib? And why did Sabby ask for juice first and then coffee? Coffee might take longer to make—maybe she wanted to be alone with Mrinal longer. Oh what the hell, I've got to take hold of myself!

She wanted a breath of air, she scolded herself. She wanted to go and see to the driver and whether he'd been sent his tea and snacks. She sat down a moment quietly on the deep cane sofa on the verandah, behind the potted palms and told herself the stern truth she'd been avoiding. Let go of him. Let go. Sooner or later, it's got to be. Suddenly she jumped to her feet, her fear out-shouting her reason: What am I saying? What the hell am I saying? She escaped into the bathroom and scanned her pale, crazed face in the mirror. The coffee would be ready, Basant had the trolley laden and Vishnu was waiting for her cue to roll it in and hand out the plates.

When she entered the room, the silence was unnerving. The album lay on the table. Sabby sat upright in her chair, looking upset. And Mrinal? Who knew anything about him now except she, Anita, and maybe Ranjit. She checked the posture of his hands and found them slack on the armrests, impassive. And she wondered what scene had just taken place here?

'A little something to go with the coffee, Sabrina?' She was surprised at the cool poise with which she spoke, as though that one moment's confrontation with an unwelcome truth had shaken and then steeled her. 'Sugar? One spoon, Vishnu. You don't like sweet things? Oh, just this once it won't harm you. Try this pista burfi—it's Mrinal's favourite. Oh, okay, let it be. Have some cheese puffs then...' Her calm self continued to amaze her and she indulged it. It was Sabby who was quiet, impenetrable. There was a troubled vibe in the air. She tried to fill the silence with her bright hostess voice:

'The 14th of July—yes, the fall of the Bastille, I remember. I made a point of visiting the Place de la Bastille when we visited Paris, but there was nothing there. I half expected some ruins or something but all I did was dive into a perfume shop and shop around, to Mrinal's great impatience.' How easily she reclaimed her husband through this narrative of domestic irritability, my memories against yours, I have them too. 'And just imagine—it's the 14th of July tomorrow? What a coincidence. I was reading that it's a historic day too, in its own little way. It's curtains down on the telegram tomorrow— did you know?'

Sabby spoke in a strained voice: 'But of course.' She put her plate carefully on the table, lifted her album and put it back in its plastic case and the bag into her shoulder bag, stood up and said : 'Well then, Mika...' She bent and kissed Mrinal on his forehead, straightened the shawl on his shoulder and gave it a little pat. 'See you then.'

Anita escorted her to the portico and saw her off. She returned to where Mrinal sat in his wheelchair and sat down in the chair beside him, looking at him a long time. Wondering what Sabby had meant by that strange loaded sentence—'But of course.' Maybe she'd been the fortunate recipient of Mrinal's telegrams too, much before she, Anita, did.

She did not have to wait longer than the next night. With a jangling of the gate and the dogs barking their heads off and the door-bell shrilling, arrived an old visitor on his ramshackle bicycle—a little old man from another age, dressed in faded khaki shirt and trousers who announced his arrival with an old, familiar call: 'Teleegram'!

Vishnu brought it in to her. It had come from New Delhi and had been sent off at 11.58 on 14-5-2013. It was 2 a.m. The typed words picked up Ben Jonson's poem where they had been left off thirty-seven years ago: The thirst that from the soul doth rise Doth ask a drink divine—STOP—But might I of Jove's nectar cup I would not change for thine—STOP—For Anita from Mrinal—STOP

She took it into his room as soon as he was awake and unfolded it before him. 'No mistakes this time, see,' she said to him, kneeling beside his bed to show it to him better. 'What an old romantic you've always been. Nothing the matter with your memory, see. You'll last a dozen years yet and we'll go on that Europe holiday again. And it's taken the Post and Telegraph Department 163 years to learn how to spell Ben Jonson's lines right, just when it's time for them to close down. Funny isn't it?'

So much like the rest of life, she thought. It took you a lifetime to begin understanding things, and just when you thought you'd got it right, it was time to obey that imperious decree STOP.

She lifted the pink sheet and placed it against her heart and held it there for him to see. A proper old-world gesture, befitting Ben Jonson's poem, befitting the old-world Eng Lit Professor who sent it via an old-world telegram. In the long years ahead, whenever her solitary life began, the message this telegram brought her was a knowledge to lay against the heart when the cold got too much to bear, when memories declared they'd brook no closure.

EIGHT

The Diary of Gyan Prakash

*T*his Gyan Prakash sure had a wacky sense of humour, whoever he was. Raju, the Coffee House's Head Waiter, had no idea as to his identity. He might have been a retired bureaucrat on a lark, corporate guy, lazy academic, has-been judge or lapsed media-man, for all he knew. He was not one of the original Coffee House regulars. He'd shown up one fine day, taken a corner table, ordered. By the time the waiter returned with his coffee and idli-sambhar, he was busy scribbling in a thick old notebook. After that first afternoon, Gyan Prakash came daily, always at the same time, and always occupied the same table and sat scribbling in the same notebook. After the first week he used to leave the notebook behind in Raju's custody and would retrieve it on arriving. Then he disappeared, just as suddenly as he had come, and never returned to claim his diary. Raju brought out the diary and spoke expansively of the writer who'd come incognito and written his sheher-nama at the corner table.

A sheher-nama it was not. More of a record of crazy kar-namas. By which I mean exploits and freewheeling high jinks in pen and ink, fuelled by a surfeit of high spirits. Written in a style echoing a certain kind of familiar British humour, found in middles and columns of the city's newspapers for about six decades of the twentieth century, it was soberly dead pan, wacky and mischievous and a sure-fire page-turner. Raju claimed he'd shown it to umpteen people who'd taken it to Agarwal's nearby and got it photocopied. Later Raju had taken to keeping himself well-stocked with photocopies for the convenience of customers who might be interested in owning personal copies. A strange and amusing instance of chamber-literature, circulating by hand. Bought for the price of a cup of coffee and a dosa. It was enough to undercut several local bestsellers! Lately it had even inspired a translator to spirited effort. And start riotous guessing games among the critical reading public. You can be sure I bought a copy on my visit to Allahabad this time and read it from its first stapled-together page to its last tantalizingly unfinished one, sitting there at the very table at which it had been written, beneath the old barred window.

It opened with ceremony and a rakish sort of panache:

'April 16, 1970. A hot sunny morning,' the chronicle began, 'a lone pastor was sighted, ambling down what used to be known as Edmonston Road but has now been rechristened Tashkent Marg. Viewed against the impressive rear of the St Joseph's Cathedral and the school alongside, there was nothing unusual about a dignified cassock-clad friar taking his constitutional. The figure was feeble, bearded, wore a sola hat and was constrained to support himself with an old walking stick. There was in his countenance the mellow righteousness that comes of a long and rewarding career, dedicated to loving his neighbour, tenderly instructing the young, and meting out unstinting severity to the wicked.

What made this particular figure extraordinary was that, some distance behind him, followed a group of raucous boys on bicycles, encouraging and cheering him on. Other odd features became manifest to the observer of this little tableau—to wit, yours truly. The good padre's behaviour occasionally lapsed to unpriestly misconduct. For example, he hailed a passing rickshaw and began asking the way to the nearest hooch bar. And, if not a hooch bar, then to an area of such ill repute that any cleric worth his cassock would blush to be seen there.

More high drama unfurled, a purely circumstantial stroke. Coming on a bicycle, pedalling slowly down the road, who should approach but a disgraced ex-student of the school answering to the name of Aga. Now this Aga bore a long and consuming hatred of padres in general and St Joseph's in particular. An embittered youth, his memory racked by foul recollections of canings and expulsion at the hands of just such a specimen as this walking pastor. Violent reprisal, assault, vengeance raised their heads in one overwhelming instant of murderous temptation. Biking up close behind the padre, Aga lifted his arm and dealt a resounding whack on the padre's frail shoulder. Imagine his shock when the padre, prompt as lightning, gave chase, uttering words of local abuse which had no business to figure in the dictionary of a man of God! Although the shock of the blow had deprived him of both his sola hat and walking stick, the padre took the fleeing youth by surprise, sprinting after him with a speed and energy that belied his advancing years. The cheering youths cheered louder, enormously tickled by the spectacle of a perspiring youth frantically cycling away with a galloping clergyman in hot pursuit.

Nor was this all. The amazing friar called at the homes of numerous students of St Joseph's and collected donations for the school, which found their way into the capacious pockets of his white cassock. It was only when he called at the house of the late Mr V. Rajamani, who taught in the English Department of the University, that the curtain fell. Mr Rajamani threw one piercing look at the bogus padre, then said with a straight face, 'I know who you are. You can take off that cassock now.'

The mock padre had no option but to disrobe. And to confess to Mr Rajamani that he had persuaded the dhobi who laundered clothes for the St Joseph's seminary, to let him have the loan of a cassock in exchange for five rupees. This padre was my good friend and an ornament to the general manager's position at an insurance company. At clubs and parties, alumni meets and get-togethers this story was told and retold amid guffaws and applause until many editions of it appeared, each crazier than the last. The three raucous youths who were his noisy cheerleaders became worthy servants of various institutions and public bodies, a corporate honcho, a professor and a chairman of a public sector company. I leave you to investigate their identities!

May-June, 1976

This incident belongs to the mid-seventies and involves some prominent Allahabadis: a some time Ambassador and Consul General, a future IG of Police, a senior insurance executive, two senior businessmen of the city, a senior CBI officer long posted at the CBI office in Delhi and a High Court judge who rose to be Chief Justice. Of course, at that time they were mostly unemployed hopefuls. The occasion was a feast to celebrate the selection of the future Ambassador in the Foreign Service. The venue was the Gupta Swimming Pool, the condition of the guests highly sozzled. The highlights of the evening included a beer guzzling contest and a spirited game of 'gend-tari' in the swimming pool, with chicken bones substituting for the ball. The guests had reached a high peak of enjoyment but the host was agitated because everyone had forgotten him and his achievement. He scolded the guests: 'Behave yourselves! Do not throw food about! Come out of that pool and put on your trousers! *I* paid for all that food! *I* got into the Foreign Service, not you louts! Who gave you permission to waste that food and spoil my image?'

Nobody heeded him. At last the party wound up. Host and guests mounted scooters and wobbled homewards. Some guests held on to other guests to prevent them from falling off. Some were emotional, in tears, broken because they had not made it to the civil services after months of pegging away, some in a state of high elation, singing, some muttering dark threats. Near the Saraswati Ghat—now known as Nehru Ghat and unfenced, descending steeply to the Yamuna's bank and densely wooded—they stopped to calm down and prepare themselves for arrival in their decorous homes.

The future CBI man went down the steep, wooded bank to answer what was in those polite times known as 'nature's call'. En route, he forgot all about the party, decided to take a short walk along the river bank, walked half a kilometre or so, then lay down on the bank and went to sleep.

The rest waited, grew anxious. With scooter headlights switched on, they searched frantically for their absent friend. Someone suggested that he'd probably slipped and fallen into the river and perished of drowning. Then, said the future Chief Justice, the body must be found and destroyed. More searching ensued. Terror had erased all trace of intoxication. The future Judge cautiously proposed cleaning away their fingerprints from the deceased's scooter. The future Ambassador wept at the prospect of losing his diplomatic career even before it had begun.

A report was planned that the deceased had not been part of the group at all. His scooter, that item of incriminating evidence, was taken and parked at the Allahabad Railway Station. The future IG Police recommended thorough cleaning of all fingerprints, etc., from the handlebars of the scooter. This done, the guilty mourners repaired en masse to the future Ambassador's house, where more weeping ensued.

Meanwhile, the absent one awoke and, finding scooter and friends vanished, trudged, cursing, to the future Insurance GM's house. It was 3 a.m. by the time he reached. He awoke the insurance man's father, ever a terrifying disciplinarian, and asked after his friends. He was informed by the stern father that no one had returned from the party. So, cursing some more, he walked home, arriving by day-break, turned in and slept, tired out after his marathon walk.

It became a matter for the intervention of fathers. The future diplomat's father telephoned the insurance man's father, who was a lawyer, to discuss the legalities of the situation. Whether in the absence of the body, Civil Service appointments ran the risk of being revoked. The latter, who had already been awoken earlier that night by the deceased, betrayed no emotion and directed the entire group of mourners to his bungalow that they might study the legal position. They arrived and were lined up by an expressionless lawyer-father. Section and clause of the Indian Penal Code were cited, fear of God and police instilled, fifty ear-held sit-ups-sit-downs ordered. All, future Ambassador, Chief Justice, corporate executive, captain of industry and IG of Police, humbly obeyed. Then they were commanded to go home and get some sleep before the police arrived for them.

But the morning brought, not the police but a phone call from the dead. An angry, abusive ghost, demanding the whereabouts of his scooter. Shamefaced, Ambassador, corporate exec, Judge, IG, and captain of industry confessed that the scooter was parked, like a lone stallion in a pasture, on the Civil Lines side of the Allahabad Railway Station.

April, 1972

Once upon a time there lived in this city of Allahabad a most ravishing maiden, the like of whom history has not known. This devastating beauty had so many applicants vying for her favour that the local sonnet-and-serenade brigade touched an all-time peak which till date has remained unmatched. One couldn't walk a step without knocking over a beau. They hung around her house, dotting the Civil Lines landscape, slack-jawed and slavering, rehearsing lines of which the general import was: Be mine, be mine! They blighted their nights and days, ruined their Civil Services and Law exams, pined away to shadows of their former selves and fought duels to prove themselves.

The beauty was not to be envied. The collective admiration of the male population left her understandably pleased but terribly confused. For having exhausted all conventional methods of declaring their passion, the tormented gentry of Civil Lines embarked on ever more extravagant antics to make an impression upon the fair maiden. The desperation and wildness of popular endeavour may be illustrated by this extreme feat, which the humble historian of this chronicle had occasion to hear from the horse's mouth—one of the horses, whose identity shall remain protected. A future Income Tax Commissioner, true to his later calling, decided to conduct a raid into the beauty's mind by a method unprecedented in human imagination. He enlisted the assistance of a callow undergraduate who from time to time played the role of flunkey to him on his various adventures. It was a daring proposal that the future Income Tax Commissioner laid before the flunkey. The idea was to climb on the shoulders of the Commissioner, peep into the beauty's chamber and make devilish faces at her through the skylight—an architectural feature with which those old British bungalows were well supplied.

Initially all went well—the surreptitious entry into the bungalow's garden, evading the attention of mali and driver and parent, the creeping advance along the bungalow's rear wall to where the beauty's chamber was known to be. The flunkey was hoisted aloft, he secured a firm hold on the bar of the skylight. He espied the beauty and the beauty, studying for her exams at a table, espied him. And just as she opened her mouth to scream, the brave Commissioner Income Tax-to-be lost his nerve, abandoned the flunkey to his fate and ignobly fled. The petrified flunkey, left dangling several feet above the ground, closed his eyes, unclutched the bar and surrendered his person to the gravitational force.

It was not a soft landing by any means. The approach of a shouting domestic did not relieve the strain. Nor the din of a roaring household up in arms. His valiant escape, squeezing through a shin-bruising hedge of henna and some nasty barbed wire fencing has made the experience a teeth-jamming speed-breaker down memory lane. The failure of Operation Skylight left both Income Tax Commissioner and flunkey embittered for life, one seeking medical relief from a suspicious, scolding GP notorious for his chastising sermons, the other sulkily adopting a hermit-like existence, pegging away for his exams, to emerge a worthy member of the Allied Services. The flunkey's aptitude with speed might have caught the eye of destiny, for he recently retired an eminent Railway elder. What the beauty made of the goblin in her skylight continues to tease the imagination of this chronicler.

May 1975

By now, it will have become evident that Allahabad University once supplied its annual consignment of Civil Servants who formed the steel frame of the Indian government. Sound, responsible, assembly-line bureaucrats, stamped and guaranteed streamlined service for thirty years and more, and no need to take them to the garage before that. The Allahabad University brand name counted for something dead serious.

This tale involves another celebration party. I repeat upon oath that all the characters in this tale are real and bear resemblance to persons living and distinguished. For reasons of delicacy and decorum, I choose to cast the cloak of obscurity on the names of the participants of this little skit.

Not another IFS, the reader will rightly protest. Too true, dear reader, incredible but true. Another IFS-wallah it was, the time being 8 p.m. circa the year 1975. The site, a narrow strip of park alongside what in the old days was known as Cosy Nook in Civil Lines. A day-old IFS man (Indian Foreign Service, not Indian Forest Service, please!) sat in the company of a green-about-the ears lecturer, later a learned Professor, a would-be diplomat and an unemployed youth who'd later adorn the Legislative Assembly of the state. The Civil Services results had just been announced. Our hero had made it. He now magnanimously ordered eight bottles of beer as a treat for his mates.

It is a sinister habit of Fate's to produce a policeman when parties in cosy public places are just beginning to warm up. And those were the polite 1970s when a voluminous unofficial code of conduct governed the behaviour of the unfortunate young. Fate repeated its irksome habit. The SO Cannington Police Station materialized before them, along with a few burly, over-zealous constables.

Said the SO: 'Now then, what have we here? Three good-for-nothing vagabonds, useless louts boozing in a public place!' And as is the affectionate way of the Indian police, he brandished his baton and uttered some choice, endearing epithets which the author blushes to repeat.

The day-old IFS man was stung, his amour-propre offended by this slight. His friends were stung, outraged.

'Jaantey nahin ho aaj IAS ka result nikla hai? Yeh aaj hi Collector Sahab ban gaye hain,' threatened the unemployed future politician.

The SO fetched the beer bottles a smart crack with his baton. 'Really?' he commented sarcastically, jiggling a quizzical eyebrow. He followed it up with a string of resounding unprintables. The vocabulary of the Indian Police, as everyone knows, is imaginative and forceful.

'It's true!' bleated the IFS man.

'It's true,' chorused his companions.

'He is your senior in the hierarchy, don't you know? Your job is in danger.'

'He'll have you fired first thing tomorrow if you forget your place!'

The SO swelled. 'Before you spin me another yarn, stand up. Pick up those bottles and empty them in the grass or I'll have the skin off your buttocks!' he commanded with dire threat. So dire that the brand-new IFS man and his mates speedily obeyed, recognizing the SO as a man who meant business.

The story got around and people said to one another: 'Now we know why the grass in that park strip alongside Cosy Nook never dries up.'

September 1977

And lest the reader runs away with the impression that the population of this city comprised future Civil Servants alone, let me hasten to mention that the population of poets far exceeded that of the bureaucrat, the shopkeeper and the lawyer. At one time in history, the city was overrun by poets, so many of them going around that it assumed the dimensions of a natural disaster and a poet-management think-tank was needed! Poets of all stripes and complexions, in Hindi, Urdu, English, Bangla and even Sanskrit jostled for space, bawled into microphones at kavi sammelans and mushairas, followed you in the streets and by-lanes insisting that you listen to their verse or hung around the Coffee House, looking melancholy and thoughtful or cynical and wry or misty-eyed as the nature of their particular category of poetry demanded. Everyone knows about the famous quarrels between Nirala and Firaq and everyone has heard of Harivansh Rai Bachchan. People pointed out the two tables at which the Progressives had sat and the Parimal group had met. People still quoted Akbar Ilahabadi and Mahadevi Verma and Sumitranandan Pant. But the horde of minor poets so incensed the Solemn Elder, a quiet sipper of coffee who only wanted to chew on his dosa in peace, undisturbed by the mellifluous voice of poesy, that he bitterly spewed out the following tale at a Coffee House harangue at which yours truly had the occasion to be present. I repeat it here as he told it. A wickedly provoking tale indeed.

'I once spent the night alone in a haunted house,' declared the Solemn Elder. 'Jeep broke down, rain pouring, road map lost. Lonely dak bungalow in the Kumaon hills, drunken chowkidar, smoky lantern. Dense jungle, jackals baying, owls hooting, bats doing whatever it is that bats do. Okay, you've got the scene. Don't ask me what happened. A family of ghosts zeroed in on me and wanted to read out their poems.

'All poets?' I cried out in alarm.

'That's right,' they told me.

'But isn't there a single healthy exception?' I pleaded.

'Some wholesome out-door-type ghoul who prefers cricket to verse? No fitness fiends?'

'This is the original dead poets' society. All fiends here,' answered the hollow voice.

When I tried to escape, the doors jammed. A walking stick zoomed up in the air. A vase sped past my head and smashed against a wall. The most scary sort of telekinesis. Six shapeless ectoplasms surrounded me. No getaway possible.

'The first poem is called...' began the hollow voice, but I wasn't going to have any of it, so I cut him short: 'That's really interesting. I got it all through sheer telepathy so you needn't bother. Great conception, perfect craftsmanship, breathtaking chiselling of the silences...'

'We take no vulgar breaths and silence is our natural medium,' the hollow voice cut me short.

'Then keep to it, I say,' I enjoined him earnestly, 'keep to it, brother. It helps the next poem creeping round your head like a mouse in the kitchen shelves, before it slinks into the open trap of vulgar breath and language and the trap snaps shut and the poet lets out a whoop and says: "Got yah!" That's poetic ecstasy for you, no?'

'You have absolutely no idea of the creative process, I am sorry to say,' said a second hollow voice. 'Poetry is emotion recollected in tranquility.'

'Ah, like the morning after a big bash when the hangover is beginning to pass,' I agreed sagely. I love baiting poets, you see.

But they obviously didn't take kindly to my observation. The last emotion I can recollect in relative tranquility is the panic of hurtling down a steep staircase and out of a creaky door into the arms of the Nepali chowkidar.

'What happened, Shaabji?' he asked.

'Something funny in there, Bahadur,' I gasped. 'Mighty big-big bhoots! Voices, shapes! I'm choking!'

'Not to worry, Shaabji,' he comforted me. 'You come and rest in my outhouse. I'll brew you some good, strong chai and recite you some of my poems. I'm a poet, Shaabji,' he confided bashfully.

The above narrative so charmed the sippers of coffee and consumers of dosas that it inspired a spirited discourse from one of our University dons. Now everyone takes pride in the fact that our Allahabad University was once called the Oxford of the East. Though lately there have been perverse dissenters who are given to citing the insulting detail that Mahatma Gandhi mischievously had the Ford that G.D. Birla gave him harnessed to an ox and called it his Ox-Ford, that one had only to look around and behold the bovine, chomping their fodder, swaying in herds, unmindful of heavy traffic, blessing the streets with fulsome benediction in steaming cow-pats. Still, argued the University don, there was no getting away from lineage, the bloodlines of an institution, the ghosts—ah yes, ghosts—of the great, glorious past. He had personally devoted years of his life working on a learned project: 'Ghosts in the Works of William Shakespeare'. Now this William Shakespeare, much beloved of Allahabad University's Eng Lit dons, had fallen under suspicion of having a ghost-writer. Oh, all the pack—Marlowe, Bacon, Mary Sidney, Edward de Vere, etc., etc., until a piece of laborious research revealed the truth—Shakespeare wrote the works of Shakespeare! But, pursued our Coffee House don, what nobody knew all along was that it was an Allahabadi who had actually written the works of Shakespeare, had been Shakespeare's ghost-writer for years. Our very own Pundit Deen Dayal. Now we all know that when Indian metaphysics, mathematics, aesthetics, what have you, were touching the stars, the Brits were painting their bodies blue and running round their meadows and moors with harpoon and hatchet. Everything they'd ever learnt or produced came from the sacred East, including the works of Shakespeare, rightly the works of Pundit Deen Dayal.

Akbar's time it was. Queen Elizabeth, the First, on the throne of England. All of us have read that the Virgin Queen received offers of marriage from the royal houses of Spain and France but few know that she received a proposal from our gallant Akbar too. The idea, as records establish, was Birbal's. The Great Mogul sent a Kashmiri carpet to the Virgin Queen and when it was unrolled in her court, presto! There appeared, neatly packed within, that Sanskrit scholar par excellence, that astrologer magnifique, that palmist without peer, Pundit Deen Dayal of Prayag, renamed Ilahabas by Akbar. Pundit Deen Dayal spoke thirty-seven languages and wrote in forty. He promptly proceeded to advance his monarch's marriage proposal and sought to read the Virgin Queen's palm and plot her horoscope. What he read therein grieved him. The Virgin would remain a stubborn spinster, a cussed feminist, and so the Great Mogul, who'd dreamt of a mighty union of cultures, might as well perish the thought. Pundit Deen Dayal dared not return to Ind to break the bad news and had to be put to some use. Fortunately a script-writer at the playhouses of London, Will Shakespeare by name, talent-spotted him and found in him the inspiration to write of the Moor in *Othello*, Shylock in *The Merchant Of Venice* and Caliban in *The Tempest*. Also, Punditji discovered in himself a growing fondness for ye olde Englishe ale and an increasing frequency of visitations from the Muse. If you read between the lines and a little to the left of the lines, you'll see his ghostly shadow busy composing. His one regret was that he'd have to be buried, not cremated when he'd finally shuffled off his mortal coil, a consummation devoutly to be avoided. But after his death his loyal friend, Will Shakespeare, contrived to enlist the services of a horde of witch-hunters, having convinced them that palmist, stargazer and horoscope plotter that he'd been, Punditji was an eminent candidate for the stake. They dug up his grave and set his remains alight, that being the civilized practice in Europe with all who were dangerously left-wing. His ashes flowed down the Avon and mingled with the boundless ocean.

The don's narrative set off an outcry in the hall, many eyes in a fine frenzy rolling from earth to heaven, calling it a tale told by a you-know-what signifying whatzittcalled, etc. Our local stand-up comedian, our great Gatsby, uprose, produced a blue pencil from his breast pocket—for he was an assistant editor with a local paper—and pronounced airily: What you've just heard is nothing! I'm tired of you angrezi-wallahs ramming your angrezi down my throat. Just the other day my phone rang and I said—Lilly-ji, kindly attend. It was a long distance call. I said—Pass it here. Yes, this is the Head Office of Swatantrata Times. How-may-I-help-you? The voice spoke in angrezi and I've sworn I won't ever ever speak in angrezi. I said—Aha, I know you, who does not know you, though for one moment I thought it was our Bachchanji. Namaskar, Shakspuri Sahab. I remember a parcel had come to us from Kasba Stratford, Vilayat. Yes, we've looked at it. Some parts need rephrasing, is my opinion. Now this long speech—be, not be, yaani ki hona hai ki nahin hona hai, savaal yeh. Okay for a film lyric but meaning no offence, Shakspuri Sahab, it's not working, not working, as we editors say. Rephrase, rephrase. I've taken the liberty of cutting out Acts Two and Three. Also wherever you have used the personal pronoun 'I', I've replaced it with 'this scribe'. Any problem there? Be reasonable—there's a market to appease. Your kind of market might have liked this rambling babble—sorry...this sustained concentration, if you like—but our kind of market...I was just saying this when ofo! The line went dead. Emotional these amateur pen-pushers!

I recall that this affront set off a lively contest, the Eng Lit don rising from his chair to take on the small-time editor in one of the great language wars of the Coffee House. In a former time Firaq and Nirala had bickered over the merits of Hindi and Urdu, now my two fellow-Coffee-Housers competed in wry mockery by mimicking one another.

'Excuse me?' challenged the don. 'I too received a phone call from someone who introduced himself as Mr K. Das. I edit our university magazine, you see, and there are all manner of entries coming in. I asked him if he was any relation to Mr Tulsi Das, but he said no. I looked over my notes and gave him my considered opinion.'

'Well, Mr Das,' I said, 'I've looked over your poem but I have reservations. How can you have a protracted unilateral communication with a cloud? Excuse me, but I feel painfully compelled to cut out exactly four-fifths of your poem. Also, why do you insist on opening each verse with "Hey Megh" or "Hey Kalyani"? And there's something wrong with the title you've chosen—"Meghdutam". We've decided to change the title to "Kalyani, Megh And Me". Then, Mr Kali Das, what this plot needs is a bit of muscle. Too soft and languishing, that's what it is. Now suppose this Megh or Cloud character stops being some sort of postman or courier lad and turns into a more…errm…robust metaphor? Recast, recast, Mr Das. Think it over—I leave you to restructure it, bearing in mind my blue-pencilled comments in the margin.'

Ah, the Allahabad Coffee House, place of sacrilege, place of pilgrimage! Where lesser mortals, ravenous for the pleasures of the mind, might sit down at the tables of the illustrious and the bohemian! To share in the buffoonery, the high seriousness, the great, resounding wrangles. Where two titanic brains sat randomly sketching and ended up designing a mighty cantilever bridge. Where insoluble conundrums in mathematics were cracked. Where literary arguments led to great intellectual feuds. Ah, the glory that was! So I sit here at my table, re-living those times, I…Gyan Prakash. I could tell you of the Professor who out-argued a famous lawyer when the latter questioned his habit of emptying the sugar-pot into his handkerchief and carrying home the sugar. I could sing of the stalwarts who rediscovered a lost civilization. But I think I'll write off those lost to history. Like my doctor friend, the eminent Super Specialist you must surely have heard of, and if you haven't it's your loss.

Those days he wasn't a Super Specialist. He wasn't even a doctor but a foot-loose student of zoology, intent on the Pre-Medical Test ahead. I remember it as if it was but yesterday. A special rain-visited morning it was, a pre-monsoon squall sending the wind riffling through the leaves. The koels sated with song and mango scent. And all one's cerebro-muscular apparatus tinglingly alive. So here I was, my brain fizzing with ideas like a just-opened soda bottle, sitting at this very table in this very hall of the Allahabad Coffee House, when who should turn up at my table but the future Specialist.

He took a concerned survey of my person. 'My God,' he exclaimed, appalled, 'how ill you look!'

His words threw me all in a tizzy 'Ill?' I scorned. '-look again, will you.'

He pulled a chair and sat down opposite me. 'No, but seriously, you're a wisp of your former self.' He went on in this vein, calling me, among other things, a pale shade from beyond, an insubstantial phantom and sundry other opprobrious things.

I was miffed. 'Hey, hang on,' I interrupted him. 'I would sincerely have you believe that nothing could be farther from me, at this point of time, than illness. Illness and I are as chalk and cheese. Strong and well and full of beans.'

He was sympathetic. 'You were always so brave. Taking your afflictions with a smile. But you can't deceive me. Tell me, does it hurt much? Since when?'

I was pretty desperate by now. 'Listen, you. Before you persuade me that I am terminally stricken, let me establish, fully, finally, that I am in the pink of health...'

He ignored me. 'Who's your doctor?' he asked.

I resumed my thread. '...and to the best of my knowledge, information and belief, no doctor has felt my pulse, stared into my eyes or jabbed me with a needle in the last two years...'

He was saddened. 'Exactly,' he sat back, 'that is the whole trouble.'

He looked at me with frank admiration. 'The strength of

the human spirit!' he sighed.

'Okay, granted that medically speaking, you're not exactly unsound, but you've got to accept the fact that you aren't growing younger. The glow has faded, the sprightly radiance...'

'Here!' I cried, stung. 'Must you put it that way?'

He was persistent. 'Our stamina is declining, our brain cells dying rapidly. In ten years, in fifteen, in twenty, where will you be?'

'In this very place—the Allahabad Coffee House. I don't know about the glow and the brain cells but my stamina's going full cylinder capacity.'

'Oh no,' he smiled knowingly.

'Oh yes!' I fretted petulantly. 'I can give you a sock in the jaw to prove my point. Nothing personal. A purely empirical demonstration.'

'That will not be necessary.' He edged away primly.

I edged away primly. Half an hour of his society and I'd be convinced that I was in a state of advanced decrepitude and all my faculties incurably blighted.

'Okay,' I said, 'let's make a deal. Let me get home and make a serious, committed attempt at falling ill. Then I'll get back to you and we'll discuss it. Give me your phone number, will you?'

There were only telephones then. The landline. No mobiles, fax, email.

Of course he became the eminent Super Specialist he'd set his heart on becoming and of course he has no time now to come to the Coffee House!

But as the foregoing exchange proves, there have been those who were out on a mission to prove me ill, or worse, unhinged. I refer to the politician who used to come for his coffee and uttapa at four-thirty every afternoon. The one who talked me into writing his biography. Those days he was only a rising politician. I applied myself to the task. Then one day I phoned and told him I'd done a handful of chapters celebrating his charisma, commending his capabilities, singing praises of his eloquence, predicting his prospects. 'Okay, okay,' he cut in. 'I get the general idea. But before you go ahead, do let me take a look at it, just in case.'

I sent him a rough draft of the six little chapters I had written. He was not pleased.

'Ha!' he blustered on the phone. 'What are these? Shameful! Have you no regard for a respectable man's image? You've made me look like a sketch by R.K. Laxman.'

'You found my style a trifle light?' I ventured, cautious.

'Light!' he swore. 'How do you expect a man to carry conviction with his constituency with a biography as absurdly flippant as this? Think. You have a serious responsibility. You are the presenter of my image to history.'

I was abashed. I apologized. 'Really sorry,' I mumbled. 'But the problem is: when I begin writing about you it's hard to be serious. I've got this inconvenient sense of humour, I know.'

'Try to overcome it,' he said in the voice of a man whose patience is sorely tested.

'How?' I demanded to know.

'Maybe you could go on a conscious humour-reducing diet?'

'Which is what?'

'Half an hour each morning reflecting on the miseries of the world. Then ten minutes each hour exercising all your negative emotions.'

I promised to do my best. I worked hard at it. He telephoned to ask after my progress.

I groaned: 'It's no good. I've written six more chapters but the harder I try the funnier they get.'

'D'you see in me such an object for mirth and laughter?' he demanded in exasperation.

'I am but a humble scribe with an attitudinal disorder,' I pleaded.

'Look,' he said. 'D'you remember what Jawaharlal Nehru did for Bachchanji? He lifted him out of the soul-destroying mire of Allahabad University politics and swept him off to Delhi with a cushy appointment. Maybe a special post can be created for you when I become a minister at the Centre.'

'Ji, mantriji,' I agreed and promised to rewrite. However, after a further six chapters I realized that my career as historian-biographer just wasn't taking off. It was hard to read through my chapters with a straight face. Obviously no cushy appointment for me. All I'm left with is a name to drop, an arch reference now and then to the friend I have in high places and the biography which for three decades now has been an on-going work-in-progress.

Not that I mind name-dropping. You should see them name-dropping for all they're worth here in the Coffee House. Day in and day out you hear conversations like this:

'My great grand-dad played chess with Motilal Nehru.'
'Mine too, and there's Jawaharlal's wedding card still lying somewhere in my house.'

'My grandmother got her face plastered by Shahnaz Hussain.'

'Nonsense! How old was your grandmother and how old was Shahnaz?'

'Shahnaz was a kid then?'

'So what did she plaster your Nani's face with? Mud and Cerelac?'

'My mother and Teji Bachchan were great pals. And Amitabh once came to pay his respects. Long before he became an actor.'

'My house is on the way to Daraganj, and my father told me Firaq Sahib was often sighted, carrying a rohu fish to fry in Niralaji's house.'

'My Amma heard Ravi Shankar give his first public performance at the Senate House. And Mahadevi Bua once gave me a painting lesson.'

Then, having exhausted their resources, they might just as often start spinning colourful yarns! Like: 'When the Declaration of Allahabad was made, by which the British Crown took over India from the East India Company, one of my ancestors covered it for an Anglo-Vernacular paper.'

'When the Viceroy visited Allahabad just after the Ilbert Bill, my great grand-uncle was one of the guests invited to the Viceroy's garden party at the Government House on Lowther Road.'

But yarns and sceptical scoffing go hand in hand here. I can imagine someone demanding: 'Which Viceroy?'

And the answer coming pat: 'Lord Lowther, of course.' This provokes riotous laughter.

'Lord Lowther? You rewriting history or what? No Viceroy by that name.'

'No Viceroy? Why, the place is fairly crawling with the

names of Viceroys—Stanely, Stratchey, Thornhill, Edmonston.'

'Rubbbish, those weren't Viceroys!' 'What were they then?'

'Chief Justices, a Commissioner, a Police Officer.'

'But Hastings, Auckland, Clive, Elgin? What were those?'

'Those were Viceroys but no Lowther, I'm dead sure.'

'Okay tell me—if Lowther wasn't a Viceroy, why wasn't he one?'

'What is it to you? Why are you palpitating to know? Was he one of your father's fathers?'

'Here, mind what you say!'

'Why, what did I say?'

'You abused my family!'

'I did not.'

'Okay, okay, pipe down,' say the onlookers to this little tableau. 'Really does it matter now? Our roads are no longer catalogues of Viceroys. Mahatma Gandhi, Jawaharlal Nehru, Sarojini Naidu, Kamla Nehru, Kasturba, Dayanand, Vivekananda—the whole brigade has put the goras to flight. It's only toadies like you who remember.'

'You call me a toady?'

'Pipe down, pipe down,' counsel the pacifists.

'Oh, we all know you come of pedigreed lineage. When the Pandavas were roaming about in exile, they sought the help of a local Prayag goonda—who might have been one of your ancestors—only the epics call him a rakshasa.'

'What?'

'And when Lord Bharat met Lord Ram near the Bharadwaja Ashram, another of your ancestors was sandal-bearer to Lord Bharat!'

'This is confusing,' protests one of the interested audience.

'Lord Bharat carried Lord Ram's sandals and Pandeyji's ancestor carried Bharat's?'

'Exactly.'

'This is gross distortion of scripture! I'll take you to court over this! Public Interest Litigation!'

'Pipe down, pipe down, Mishra!' roar the delighted onlookers.

'I'm serious,' scowls Mishra.

'Look,' interrupts one chuckling spectator, who might actually be me: 'I have a better idea. Let us float a Prayagvarta Association, membership open to all local descendants of characters from mythology and history. We'll make Pandey President and Mishra Secretary.'

'One minute,' cries Mishra, 'first, how does one prove descent? Second, I insist on being President and let Mishra be Secretary.'

'Objection, milord,' guffaws Pandey, 'a simple affidavit from the Kutcherry is all that's needed to meet the first requirement; and as for Presidentship, let us have a Coffee House election and canvas around and then we'll see.'

'Raju, six masala dosas and six coffees!' calls out another convulsed onlooker.

'Let Pandey buy his votes. Starting now!'

So now you know why I love this place and can't bear to leave it. But leave it I must, slowly wending my way to the Station on my rickshaw, my final self-indulgence. For this Allahabad rickshaw is a contraption created for a leisured society, one that does not need to lash itself into a tearing rush. That does not have to attempt unnegotiable distances. That was made for people who did not insist on fastidious insulation from heat or cold and who inhabited an environment that was charmingly innocent of pollution. In other cities the cycle-rickshaw is a metallic thing in which the passenger is propped at a precarious angle, the feet resting on a narrow ledge and the hindquarters perilously upheld by a slippery rexine seat. And the hood too is an option rather to be foregone than adopted. But the Allahabad rickshaw has a secure floor, a rectangular plank of wood on which the feet may dispose themselves as comfort dictates, the seat a flat, steady bench on which the passenger may plant himself as in an armchair. And the hood opens its sheltering pleats above the head with the courteous generosity of a state umbrella. The slow turn of the wheels sets up a restful thought rhythm so it is easy to understand why the late Professor Y. Sahai of the University when urged to buy a car protested that he valued his rickshaw rides because all his quality thinking was done then.

So I see myself riding to the Allahabad Junction, readying myself to travel from one time-grid to another, thinking, ah Allahabad, how do I love thee, let me count the ways. I love the Allahabad chaat and the Loknath rabri and the Khusraubagh guava and the Coffee House banter. I love the buff-colured stone of the All Saints' Cathedral and its sacred, soaring interior. The shady silence of the Public Library. The sheet of the Yamuna seen from Mankameshwar Temple with the sound of bells carrying across the waters. The foggy winter lights on the new bridge. The dim lamps burning on the white mazars of Company Bagh and the koel-song in the Bagh's mango groves. The spray of pigeons arching up from the red tiles of the Senate House and their cruising descent on the carved kiosks and cornices of the English Department.

The orchestra of colours behind Ghantaghar. And the wheels of the train on Phaphamau Bridge, rumbling out a familiar drumbeat. And below, the long sandy, moonstone-white drape of water that is the Ganga.

Far away, in another corner of the planet, in an airport lounge of Kuala Lumpur or San Francisco, two CEOs might find themselves sitting next to one another and each might recognize the other's face from long ago. Suddenly one might lean across and ask: 'Mumfordgunj?' To which the other might answer, instantly in sync, 'No, George Town.' For Allahabad creates instant chemistry between people who left and never returned. The first might ask: 'Sir Sunderlal Hostel?' And the second might respond, 'No, Muir.'

Gyan Prakash's diary ended abruptly but he probably wished to let his connection with the city remain a suspended conversation to be picked up just as he left off whenever chance or nostalgia brought him to Allahabad again.